miss corpus

Annie—
God damn.
Here we go...
Happy readings—
CMC
Jan. 29th,
2003

Also by the author

rest area

miss corpus

Clay McLeod Chapman

AN IMPRINT OF HYPERION
NEW YORK

Library of Congress Cataloging-in-Publication Data

Chapman, Clay McLeod.
Miss corpus / Clay Chapman.—1st ed.
p. cm.
ISBN 0-7868-6738-8
1. Automobile travel—Fiction. 2. Traffic accidents—Fiction. 3. Southern States—Fiction. 4. Loss (Psychology)—Fiction. 5. Grief—Fiction. I. Title.
PS3603.H36 M57 2003
813'.6—dc21 2002032807

Hyperion books are available for special promotions and premiums. For details contact Hyperion Special Markets, 77 West 66th Street, 11th floor, New York, New York 10023, or call 212-456-0133.

FIRST EDITION

10 9 8 7 6 5 4 3 2 1

for my mother

m i s s   c o r p u s (point of origin)

s o u t h b o u n d

v i r g i n i a

william colby

n o r t h   c a r o l i n a

tollbooth buddy: wallace reese

william colby

s o u t h   c a r o l i n a

tollbooth buddy: audrey dow

william colby

the henley road motel: ted henley

william colby

n o r t h b o u n d

f l o r i d a

philip winters

the mourning glory group

g e o r g i a

philip winters

the mourning glory group: I on you

philip winters

s o u t h   c a r o l i n a

the mourning glory group:

ward and wendy raymond

philip winters

m i s s   c o r p u s (point of impact)

miss corpus

Read, for this is my body. Take the distance between Virginia and Florida—a long-sprawling spine of states connected by I-95—and then you have the backbone to me. Each town along the way serves as its own vertebra, notch for notch, winding down the coastal road with the weight of five states upon my shoulders. Think of every back road that breaks off from my highway as a rib, curving out into the countryside, protecting every vital city within its grip—giving support to the South. What puts meat onto these streets are the people who drive through, their commute the very marrow of my bones. My lifeblood is made up of road trips, my heartbeat founded upon family vacations, Greyhound buses, joyrides. I'm alive for as long as you're driving. So come on down, honey. Pay me a visit, please.

That road map of me has been in your glove compartment for years, now—hasn't it? That snapshot was taken ages ago. I used to be the pinup girl of this country. Miss Southern States. Every tourist in America has that centerfold hiding in their car, somewhere—either crumpled up underneath their seat or stuffed in between the cushions. Whoever's stuck navigating will pull that picture out, ogling over my body for miles, simply searching for the right road to steer for—only to fold me up the wrong way once they're done, creasing my image until I look more wrinkled than I already am. You can't even recognize me there, lying right alongside the Atlantic—my body bending slightly at the hip, my left leg stretched out, my foot dipping into the water. I've grown older since then. Developed in different places. There are pit stops that've cropped up along my body that will never make their way onto a road map, *ever*—while other blemishes have been bulldozed away for good. A little nip and tuck to save face for the tourists. Give them something to come back for next summer.

Once you hit North Carolina, take a glance out through the window of your car for me. You'll find miles worth of forest there, a wooded flesh lush enough to wrap you up inside (*if* you were to pull over). That's where my skin's the smoothest—where you could walk on for hours and never find a break in these trees, getting lost along the way. In me. There are paths hidden within that're barely walked on by anyone. Not anymore, at least. Whenever someone hikes through, it's such a caress across untouched territory, it tingles. Even tickles me. It feels as if a hand is passing down my lower back, a single finger gliding along the arch of my spine—gently dipping into that ditch where my hips begin and the hills take over. The number of times I'm touched there is so rare, these backwoods empty and numb of anyone nowadays, that I'm left alone, yearning for somebody to just walk through me.

I've had to reduce myself to roller coasters, you know—just to tempt these vacationers into visiting me. I've been forced into putting on a pair of mouse ears, having my picture taken with obnoxious children all day—when I used to be so much more than this. These people simply buy their T-shirt of me and head home again, snap off a few photos to prove to their neighbors that they'd made the trek.

Well, let me save you the trouble of nosing around. Dig your hands into me and they're going to come back black, I promise. The ground down here has roasted over into coal, making life a slow burn for me. Centuries. I flirt with the tourists, just to pass the time. After coughing on their car's discharge all day, I have to admit, the fumes I've inhaled are habit forming. These mufflers have become an iron lung for me, smoking a pack and a half of exhaust pipes every day. My cigarette's lit with a flick of the ignition—these husbands slipping me a wink with their turn signal just before they head back onto the highway.

Toodi-loo. Come back soon, sweetheart.

Still hiding some charm, somewhere.

So I'm growing older. So I'm not what I used to be, *fine*. Don't think for an instant I don't know my hips are being whisked off into the ocean after every high tide. No surprise, there. The waves have been whipping at my waist for so long now, my hips have given up—my shoreline slipping away from the rest of me, widening my thighs. But when I was in my prime, I spurred more men into red jealousy than any other lady around. Wars were fought over me. That's how beautiful I used to be. (Let's not forget our history, now. All right?) Boys would take a bullet into their hearts for me, valiantly ushering in their own death—because they believed their heart would break if they were to lose my love. They would rather die for me than let their land go. And I loved them for it. I made them proud. I soaked up the blood of hundreds into my skin and it left me young. *Ravishing*. I wore their bodies like jewelry—a necklace of dead confederates at my chest, a ring of corpses wrapped around every finger. My honor was upheld by enough suitors to send every state into envy, *pure* yellow-eyed envy—all of these other girls just jealous of the pride imparted upon me. Because I was the embodiment of one's love for their country. I was patriotism at its purest.

I was the lay of a nation—and don't you forget it.

From sea to shining sea.

Not much blood's shed for me now. The soldier boys have all been drained, the bullet holes tapped dry—leaving my cheeks pale and deprived. I barely doll myself up anymore. Nobody would notice, even if I did.

I've had to hock my wares, just to get by. All these treasure-hunters keep coming through, digging up whatever artifacts of my past they can find. Robbing me blind of my history. People even want to take my states away. If I overhear one more tourist jabber on about how Virginia isn't *really* a part of the South, I swear I'll cause an earthquake. They call it the heart of the Confederacy for a reason, people. There's a pulse beneath your feet, radiating through the rest of this country. More bodies have been buried into me than anywhere else, weighing me down with the heft of humanity. So many men, I'm surprised I haven't fallen off into the ocean yet. Just broke off from the rest of the country and drowned.

But I've survived. I've outlasted everything that's been built upon me, watching the whole country crumble—like an unfortunate mother who outlives her own children. I'll be here long after you're gone, you can bet on that. Tell me: When it's finally time for you to lay down your life, and they bury you—just where do you think it is that you'll be going?

Right here. Right into me.

Motherhood's been reversed for me. God's given me the graves of men, impregnating me with the dead—a swarm of bodies swimming through this soil; all of them tunneling toward the core of me, searching for their fertile purchase. None of them ever make it. They all give up after six feet.

We keep trying though, me and Him—and we're going to get it right, one of these days. We're at it all the time. I barely even stand up anymore. I just stay here, lying on my back. Waiting for Him. That man's a fountain for funerals—that's for sure. Showers me with a downpour of corpses every day. My belly's overflowing with dead bodies. I can feel them inside, their warmth fading within me fast—that tiny trickle slipping down my leg, puddling up into swampland. All it's going to take is for just one of them to reach in deep enough, burrow down into the ground until they tap at the very center of me. I'll take over from there.

You just wait and see how swollen South Carolina becomes in a couple months. Highways will shift. Asphalt will crack. These mountains are going to overflow with milk, once I start lactating. The lakes will surge up, cupping their water like a navel cradling sweat—dribbling down the side of my stomach in a flood. You wait and see what becomes of this country. I'm going to give birth to a new continent, baptized in the Atlantic. It'll be a girl. A beautiful baby daughter that I can spoil rotten. She'll grow up to be everything that I couldn't. That I can't. And she'll have blue eyes, two pale ponds of water that will always look toward me with love.

I'm supposed to be the page that holds history—and it's become lonely. Somewhere, someone decided that the ground was as good a text as any, tattooing the memoirs of men within my skin. These dead bodies have become letters to a fleshly alphabet, their skeletons spelling out worm-ridden words—the rows of graves stretching out into sentences that document their very existence. But I tell you, these cemeteries stink of rotten writing. Whoever had the bright idea of making me the manuscript of humanity probably hadn't paid me a visit in a long while. Look at me now. When you're the pulp that makes the page in which history's written, what are you supposed to do when you begin to age? When your corners crumble and your skin yellows? What should you do when the very words that constituted the past fade from your flesh, the paper stale and brittle enough to break under your own fingers?

Don't I deserve to be preserved? I want to write my body down. Scribble it on something that's going to keep—because at this point, I've survived longer than the books that were written about me, living past all the printed matter. Their pages are as feeble as people. They rot. There's nothing to a composition that doesn't decompose on its own, this paper as flimsy as flesh.

And this is what I'm supposed to rely on? My life is going to rest in some text, some encyclopedia that'll crumble apart in a couple years? I want something stronger than that. I want something eternal.

I'll need a new map of myself. One that's going to ensure me some longevity for my legacy, a breath beyond my own. You want to know about me? My life's an open book. So go ahead and get reading.

southbound

virginia

Good morning, everybody. It's seven A.M. on a Thursday morning. Nelson Lennon back again with your morning report. Traffic's looking pretty good from here to Petersburg, save for some slight congestion just off of I-95 at the Powhite Parkway. If you're traveling south on 64, you might want to steer clear of the Williamsburg exit. There'll be road construction going on throughout most of the afternoon—probably on into tomorrow morning. The weather today will keep itself steady in the high seventies. Clear skies and a high humidity count for the rest of the week. Hope it stays that way until Sunday. Until tomorrow, have a good one, everybody . . .

william colby

Johnny Appleseed's an uncle *of yours, William.*

Nothing can bring as much excitement to a little boy as telling him he's kin to a tall tale. Those were the exact words that came out from my mother's mouth the moment I told her who we'd learned about in class that day. *On your father's side of the family,* she said. *Didn't your dad ever tell you that?*

How great does he go back? I asked.

Oh, he'd have to be a great-great-great-great-uncle by now. Six or seven generations at least.

Maybe it was because I still had my backpack on—the bulk of books weighing down my shoulders—but for a second there, I felt as if I was going to faint. My knees weakened over the idea that there was a link between me and history, a relative that endured time by simply sowing seeds through the countryside. Wait until the kids at school heard about this. There was royalty within my blood. My family tree just so happened to have apples on it, thanks to John Chapman. Born in Massachusetts, he spent over half a century on his bare feet, roaming through the northwest before it ever sectioned off into states. When settlers started to roll in, they were greeted with the sight of my uncle's orchards—the smell of apple blossoms welcoming them to their new home. He made a legacy for himself with over a million seeds. If you were to bite into an apple back in the early 1800s, chances are it would've come from one of his trees. Two hundred years later and a spare number of them still bear fruit—which was why I begged my mother to make a special trip to the grocery store for me, stocking up on as many apples as our cart could hold. Digging my teeth into a Granny Smith had resonance now. I was supporting my family's dynasty with every swallow.

Johnny Appleseed isn't real, my best friend had said. *He's just someone somebody made up to make us eat apples.*

But he's a relative of mine, I said.

And Paul Bunyan's your cousin? You got Babe the Blue Ox in your family, too?

The only way I figured I could prove my heritage was to hit the road, showing my friends that sowing seeds was in my blood. My heart swelled with a sense of sovereign responsibility, as if it was my duty to continue my uncle's work. I uprooted every book from my backpack, filling it up with as many apples as I could carry. I decided to head down South, walking as far as Florida—eating my luggage along the way. My wake would open up into an orchard, a string of trees lining along the highway. I'd make my great-great-great-great-uncle proud, knowing I'd picked up his business exactly where he'd left off—finishing off the rest of America. There wouldn't be a corner of this country that didn't have our legacy growing out from its soil.

I ran away right after school, walking as far as fifteen blocks before getting lost. My sense of direction wasn't as sharp as

Johnny's—my inner compass was spinning around so fast, I got dizzy simply watching the cars rush past. I couldn't tell which way was home anymore. My back was beginning to ache from all those apples. I looked hunchbacked, carrying that much fruit—a dozen humps rolling over my shoulders. My teacher had told the class how Johnny would walk for miles every day, stopping off at a stranger's house to rest. He passed through five states on his feet, while I never made it out of my own hometown. I got as far as five miles beyond my front door, ending up huddled in some ditch just off the highway. Our teacher told us that a tall tale is a story that's rooted within a real event, a fact that's been passed from one mouth to another, embellished the more it's told, for so long, it eventually loses its truth. My great-great-great-great-uncle John Chapman had evolved into Johnny Appleseed after years worth of word of mouth, his legacy spreading into legend the longer folks spoke of him. All I wanted was to become a tall tale right then, feeling the need to remove myself from the reality of being lost, leaving a facsimile of who I was in my place. I didn't want to be William Colby just then. I didn't want to be seven years old, with nothing but a bookbag full of fruit on my back. I wanted to be little Willie Appleseed. I wanted to cross the state line before my mom worried over where I was, a trail of apple trees lining up behind me, showing me how to get back home.

Twenty years later and my compass is still cracked. Seems as if I end up getting lost no matter where I want to go. Having a car hasn't helped much. I don't even know which direction I'm heading in, anymore. There's going to be an aneurysm on this interstate—all these cars clotting up behind me—if you don't tell me where I am right now. I'm not driving out of this tollbooth until I know what state I'm in. I've sunk through enough of this country to know I'm not any higher than North Carolina. I keep drifting away at the wheel. That's my problem. Woke up in the

Wal-Mart parking lot not too long ago. I hadn't even gotten past pulling the keys free from the ignition. The running engine kept lulling me out to sea, sleep reaching for me every time I'd shut my eyes—only to find the kitchen hiding behind my lids. The floor was baring its tiles at me, clenched teeth under my feet, the linoleum wanting to swallow me whole.

Shopping carts went wobbling by, sounding as weak as my knees, all of them staggering under the strain of their groceries. The wheels were flickering over the pavement, like chains rattling at my ears. Thought I was listening to the anchor lowering again, shattering through the ocean. Bringing me home. The muscles in my legs are rubbery after months of standing over the ocean. The ache was still in them when I pressed my foot down onto the brake. My ankles kept recollecting my first step onto solid ground, the shock of earth absorbed into my body—the queasy feel of sturdy dirt swelling up into my stomach.

Shelly had waited until I shipped off before pulling out the maps, taking the past four months to chart out our week on the road. Our kitchen table was littered with over a dozen atlases, covering the surface in a tangle of interstates—as if the varnish had been skinned, exposing a tapestry of veins laced through the wood. When I had first walked into the kitchen that day, duffel bag still in hand, I thought I'd entered into a morgue for furniture—the bare blue and red highways stretching over the chairs, the countertop. There wasn't an inch to our kitchen that hadn't been dissected by one of her charts.

Shelly'd been learning up on the anatomy of the road. She'd spent four months studying all the freeways and interstates running along the coast, until there wouldn't be a back road that she didn't know where it led to, where it could take the two of us.

"All you're in charge of is loading up the car," she'd said to me, just before I left. "When you get back, you're going to have to buy us one of those huge coolers. I'm not eating fast food for a week. By the time we got to Florida, I'd be as fat as one of those . . . those fat things. What do they call them?"

"What things?"

"The whales they have down there. The albino ones."

"Manatee?"

"*Those*. I'll look like a manatee if I end up eating at every McDonald's we drive past."

Pressing the buckle at my waist, the seat belt lashed across my chest, zipping over my neck in one last lick. Reminded me of kisses Shelly used to whip me with. Her tongue could coast over my skin so fast, she'd lay down a strip of saliva, like a tire peeling off its rubber across pavement. Now all I had was nylon.

First thing I had to do was buy some of those coolers. For Shelly.

The shop's automatic doors peeled back. Hollow songs tinkled over my head, the music barely there—just audible enough to sound like someone humming at my ear. It could've been Shelly's lips releasing a lullaby.

Having been at sea for so long, all of the everyday objects I found myself surrounded by suddenly felt foreign to me, altering into products I couldn't even recognize anymore. They had these inflatable baby pools stacked on top of each other, all empty and neatly folded, looking like a wall of rubber lungs. The picture on the packages was just egging my breath on to blow them up. I read the disclaimer, the warning nearly lost on the box's side. *Two inches of water is a sufficient amount to drown a child. Please do not leave young children unattended when swimming.*

I'd left Shelly alone for four months, not even enough to count past the fingers on one hand.

"You'll be back by the time you reach your ring finger," she said. "Start counting the months at your thumb, so once you get to your wedding band, you'll be coming back to me."

An officer once told me to *never underestimate a body of water, Will, whether it's the Pacific Ocean or a puddle you just pissed up.* Men who were lonely enough could drown in their own tears, choking on their sobs so no one else in the bunk could hear them. Men on deck were drowning all the time, he told me, whether they were up to their eyeballs in the ocean or not.

Which is why I thought I should buy a few inflatable armbands. There was a rack of pullover life preservers, all of them packaged in this clear plastic wrapping. I'd had days at sea when just a little bit of air wrapped around my arms would've come in handy. Wondered why the merchant marine never gave their sailors a pair to put on while working on the water. I pictured all the men on deck wearing their own, the colors popping up all over—pink, baby blue, purple. There'd be a picture of a dolphin or a whale winking over each bicep, like temporary tattoos for a softened sailor.

You should've seen the shelves where they kept the coolers, stacked seven boxes tall and five deep. At the top were the soft assortment—these handhelds made with this nylon material similar to seat belts. Gloves for soda pops. Playmate had their own special brand of cooler, made with red and white plastic. Candy-cane colors. There was a button centered on its side, keeping the lid sealed shut. When it opened, the inside of the cooler let out a breath of manufactured plastic. At the bottom were all the Igloos, the biggest coolers they had in stock. This brand had the lid resting on top, hinged at one side. A thin rubber lining ran around the brim, like a mouth determined to seal the cool air in. When I opened one, I could hear the padding peel apart—a tender rip between lips. The inside went deep. A foot and a half, at least.

"You must be planning one heck of vacation, sir," the boy behind the register said. His voice cracked under *vacation.* When I looked at him, I lost myself in his acne. His face was lumped up with pockmarks. Reminded me of what it looked like to watch the setting sun lay down a red glow over the ocean, the sea slightly rippling under the ruddy color.

"Come on, Will. Make me a widow," Shelly'd said to me, pulling the covers over our heads—a flash flood of cotton washing over the bed, burying our bodies under a murk of sheets. "If you drown out there without marrying me first, what am I going to do? Mouth off about some boy I was supposed to wed? That's not how it works. You got to give me more than that. A dead fiancé fades away once the next guy comes around. But if you were a husband, *my husband,* then I'd have more to mourn over. You know?"

She had her chin inching across my chest, drifting up to my shoulder—like an air bubble rolling over my skin.

"*'Yeah, he was my boyfriend. We were going to get married when he came home . . . but he never did.'* Sounds awfully dull to me. But what about this—" Pushing aside some phlegm, her throat shifted into a lower chord. "*'We'd just wed. Said "I do" right before he set sail. Had to hold off on our honeymoon until he returned. That way, he'd have something to look forward to when he came home. I'd have the trip all planned out by the time he came back. But he never did. Now I'll never shake him. . . . I keep his ring on my finger to remember him by. . . . 'Cause I know he's still wearing his, wherever he is under that ocean. . . . Which means we'll be married until the end of time in his little waterlogged mind. . . . I'm staying faithful to the man, until I die.'*"

"So, you want to get married now, then?" I asked. "Is that what you're saying, here?"

"Uh-huh." She kissed me at my shoulder.

"Even though I have to leave soon?"

"Uh-huh." A kiss at the curve in my jaw, right below the ear.

"Two months from now, you know. I'll be gone for four."

"I know, I know." A nibble at my ear. Holding the lobe in between her teeth, she flicked her tongue across my flesh trapped inside her mouth.

"And *then* you want me to drown?"

She bit me, giving up on talking. Pressed her mouth into the run of my throat, the pressure peeling her lips open until her teeth tapped at my jugular—my pulse swelling against the broadside of her incisors. She pinched the skin, lifting a sliver up between her teeth. My neck cricked into the sting. . . .

And in that flinch—I was inside the car again, driving home. My throat had been sanded down by the seat belt, the nylon licking the wound it'd made earlier that afternoon. Looking in the rearview mirror, I found myself chauffeuring a half dozen coolers, stacked up evenly in the backseat. Our home is nothing more than a two-floor rental. Our landlady's been wilting away in some retirement home for years now, fed off of the money we pay every month. She won't sell it to us because it's holding too many memories for her—even if she's not fit to live there alone, anymore. We couldn't afford it, anyhow.

The lid of our mailbox was forced open from too much stuffing—like a jaw locked in an awkward yawn, gagging on a week's worth of letters and magazines. A pile of rain-soaked newspapers had disintegrated into the grass. Each paper was rolled up into itself, sinewed by a rubber band that had begun to slice through its own skin. Each wet cylinder was decomposing over the top of the newspaper from the day before. A chronological rot, as if old bones were blending into one another.

Shelly had promised to pick me up at the docks that afternoon. I had sifted through all the couples, pushing away every other family hugging their boy, in hopes of finding her at the other side, locking eyes with her, watching her head bob over the shoulders of everyone else.

Getting lost in the throng reminded me of when I first set off to sea. Two years before and fresh out of high school. I had a couple days to convince Shelly to make the leap over from senior-year sweethearts to the big commitment with me. Make me a real boyfriend.

"I've got a year in my favor, already. Right? That's more time between us than any other relationship I've ever been in."

"Me, too."

"So four months shouldn't be such a hassle, right?"

"Maybe. I don't know."

"I'm coming right back. You won't even know I'm gone."

"But you will be gone, Will . . ."

"Think about it this way: I got a job already, right out of school. I'm not flipping hamburgers or working a nine to five. I've got a chance to work for four months solid, and then take off for the next couple weeks—which gives us enough time to make up for however long I'm gone. We won't have to get out of bed for a month straight."

"What if you fall overboard?"

"I'm not going to fall overboard."

"What if you drown on me? How would I know what happened to you?"

"I won't even get near the water, I promise."

"If I'm waiting with your father on the dock, then that'll be all the answer you need—won't it? Pine hard enough and see what happens."

The next four months of my life were divided between the sea and the shore, feeling this rift within my own rib cage—a gap spanning the Atlantic. I turned nineteen out over the ocean. Didn't tell a single sailor on board about it. Simply celebrated my birthday with nobody but one big body of water. I kept on deck when most boys headed in for supper, looking for some solace in the water. What I'd find most nights was just the sea snuffing out the sun, dragging all the light under the surface and drowning it. My mind kept turning back to shore, wondering about what-if's like a coin flipping around in my skull. Heads, Shelly was waiting. Tails, I was alone already and didn't even know it.

At night, the boys would all pull out their photos of their girlfriends, competing with one another for the prettiest catch. To make it fair, we agreed that we'd line up our pictures alongside one another when no one was looking, keeping each girl in anonymity over whose was whose. Each night, someone else always won. The contest was there to keep morale up, I guess. If there was a new beauty queen each time, *Miss Merchant Marine*, every boy had something to pine for when the lights went out. Something to help push them through the next few months. When everyone was tucked into their bunks, you knew where the winner had planted his hands. He would've earned the rub for that night and no one could complain over having to hear it, knowing that their triumph might be tomorrow. It was only a matter of time before everyone would win.

Once, after a month of sea, this one sailor, Tim Peters, realized somebody wasn't tossing their picture in. "We got ten guys in this bunk and only nine pictures. Thought we agreed we'd all throw in. Unless *one of us* thinks their girl is better than all of the rest."

"My girl hasn't won in over a week—so I want to know who's not throwing in."

The only photo of Shelly that I had with me was this picture of her when she was just six years old. When I had asked for a photo of her to take along with me, she asked, "Where are you going to put it?"

"Over my bunk, I guess."

"So all of those other men can ogle over me? No way."

"Oh, come on Shell. It's important. What am I going to have to remember you by while I'm gone?"

What she gave me wasn't what I'd been expecting.

"Can I have something more recent? Like, within the last few months?"

"This will do just fine."

"How old are you here?"

"Not old enough to give those other boys the wrong idea."

After just a month, there was already a crease running down the middle of the picture—mangled from so much maneuvering between my wallet and hand. A scar ran across her throat, the fold just under her chin.

"Is it you, Colby?" Tim called out. "I thought your girl was that black-haired dog from last week. The one with the pigtails."

"Hey, asshole!" A well-worn *Playboy* shuttled across the room, the ragged pages flapping through the air. Miss October slapped Tim on the back. "That's my girlfriend!"

"So you dating a prom queen, Will? A movie star? You think you got something so special, you can't share it with the rest of us? Throw her in." Tim turned away, wanting to keep the game pure by following the rules. Fair and square or not—by this point, everyone had gotten so familiar with the pictures, it would've been pretty obvious whose photo was mine, simply from finding the new face within the old lot.

The row of photographs stretched across the floor. The soft faces of each boy's girlfriend lined up alongside the others, smiling, patiently waiting to start the contest. This was the crinkled beauty pageant played over and over, every night. The edges of each photo had frayed from so much judging. Most pictures had been snapped for nights just like these, the girls wanting to give their boyfriends something extra special to remember them by, grabbing the camera with eyes intent on keeping their men while they were away, keeping them company whenever we were at our loneliest. Plain girls were asked to pose provocatively. Homely girls had been begged for one naughty wink. The most frequently picked picture was of this one girl, naked as far as any of us could tell—her strawberry blonde hair stroking a pair of bare shoulders. The lower edge of the photo cut off just at her chest. If there had been an extra inch to the picture, we all believed we would have had a perfect view of her breasts. We were left to imagine what was below the edge of the photo, conjuring up the size, the color, the width of her nipple.

Sometimes, our imagination would get the best of us. After hours' worth of scrutiny one night, this sailor said he discovered the upper tip of this girl's left nipple. "It's there! I see it! I see it! I can really see some of this girl's tit!" The picture was passed around the room a dozen times. Each boy's palm was spread with sweat, buttering up the image with their pent-up perspiration.

"Is it there?"

"I can't see a Goddamn thing—"

"It's there, I know it! I found that nipple! It's mine! It's all mine!"

"All of you bastards better let go! I'm going to kill you if she comes back all ripped up." When the photo finally came back to her boyfriend's hands, the emulsion along the bottom edge had been worn down to the paper, a patch of white unearthed, the breast completely rubbed off. If the nipple had ever really been there, it was lost now.

So it was my turn to add to the fun. I placed Shelly's picture down right next to that blonde, stepping back so all the other boys could pile in. They nearly leaped over each other for the opportunity to see new skin, a fresh face among a month's worth of tired choices. But staring up at the pack was Shelly's six-year-old smile, her lips pulled back far enough to bare a gap in her upper front teeth.

When the boat rubbed its hull up against the dock three months later, I hopped off in a tidal wave of eager bodies. All the sailors leapt for a shoreline formed by our own families. The crowd had been standing on the dock for hours, waiting for the ship to come in sight.

Once I found my father, I saw that he was standing alone.

"Where's Shelly?" I asked. He just looked back at me, his face as ashen as ever. The hope that had kept my chest buoyant abruptly sunk. I'd been floating on the faith that she would've been there, the last four months of my life fading away.

"Where is she?"

"I haven't seen her. I came alone."

Suddenly my eyes were swallowed up by familiar palms. I'd cupped a bit of it before, squeezed some of that skin just before boarding the SS *Farewell*—only to feel the warmth of it around my eyes, sealing me into a welcome darkness.

Shelly's chin settled on my shoulder, a whisper creeping into my ear. "Guess who's still got himself a girlfriend, William Colby?"

I spun around so fast, I simply pivoted under her grip, keeping her chin at my neck. Facing each other now, the few inches between our lips were left empty of anything other than our own breath, each inhaling the other's exhale. Guess I had myself a girlfriend after all.

I've missed her voice. Being able to kiss her while she was talking, tasting her breath, the vibrations of her words running through my cheeks. If there was a way to trap a sensation like that, find out how to funnel the feeling and keep it forever—I would've tried. I would've jarred it up and taken it with me whenever I left. I took the cassette out of our answering machine just before leaving our house. I've been listening to her message here in the car's tape deck over and over again. She tells me to leave my name and number at the sound of the beep, only for the tape to flip over and ask again. *Please tell us the day and time you rung up and we'll return your call as soon as we get back. Will and me will be out of town until August. On our honeymoon.*

Now all I have are these coolers. Melted ice makes for a cheap imitation of her teeth chattering. The slosh of water running up the inner wall of these Igloos sets me off to sea again, dragging me back on board the SS *HauntMeAllOver*. I'd been buried within the bowels of that boat while everyone else slept. Manning the evaporator flats left me in charge of the ship's fresh water, making me one of the most valuable men on board. Second only to the captain, practically—if any of the other sailors even remembered that I was working below them in the first place. Since I worked the nights alone, most men began forgetting me after the first month.

The process went like this: Ocean water gets lapped up into the ship and funneled through a boiler system, the heat squeezing the salt out from the sea. The condensation is then strained, collected, and distributed through the several pipes lining the inside of the ship's underbelly—routed to showers, faucets, sinks. What the men drank passed through my hands first. Every drip, every sprinkle, every trickle. My duties began at midnight, just so that the others could have their fresh water in the morning. I'd have to keep myself awake all through the night just to read the gauges, adjust the valves, transfer good water to all the essential locations, taking on additional seawater to condense and maintain voluminous records.

Digesting. I was in charge of working the stomach of this ship.

I would crash into my cot when most men were just waking up. "See him?" a sailor would ask, elbowing one of the younger crewmen, "that's the guy they got working the flats down below."

Nobody had wanted this job. I even surprised myself, taking it. Before becoming a water tender, I'd spent my first four trips out to sea as a wiper in the engine room—mopping up oil spills with five other boys. We'd slop through puddles six inches thick, my socks soaked in engine sweat, staining my feet a deep black. There was more money in maintaining the evaporator flats than swabbing the deck or mopping the mess hall or wherever else you could earn an extra buck on board. Enough money to take your newlywed wife on one hell of a honeymoon when you got back on land. And for what? Checking gauges, flipping dials. Monkey's work that paid better than the rest of the rigors of the ship. Only thing I'd have to struggle with were the late hours. Companionship was narrowed down to the sound of my own voice—but even talking to myself was nixed, the hammering of the evaporator's engine drowning out every other sound around me. I would force myself to find Shelly in those moments, imagining her when there was nothing left for me to do. Most men on board taped up those photographs of their girlfriends wherever they worked, pasting them onto pipes that they frequently passed. But for me, a water main would bend at an angle my mind could mold into Shelly's arm, hooked over at the elbow. Certain sounds could convince me she was standing right at my back, making the noises herself. The hissing pipes spilling steam over my shoulder sounded so similar to the air that slipped out from between her teeth. If I stood close enough, the mist even reminded me of her warm breath at my neck, calling up a crop of sweat over my skin.

This was my solace, night after night. Welcoming Shelly into my shift. Better than reading the same magazine three nights in a row. A book would lull me off to sleep after the second page, the words melting into a swirl of ink.

It took me a couple weeks worth of packratting *Playboys*—but by the end of my third month, I began cutting and pasting centerfolds onto the flats. The pipes were hot enough to solder the underside of each piece of paper onto itself, no need for glue or tape to cleave the two together. Instead of simply sticking an entire photo onto the wall, I'd decided to follow the structural flow of the water mains by composing the pipes into limbs of their own. I'd place a curving arm wherever I could find the right angle, making sure that each body part matched the shape of metal beneath it. I amassed every similar limb, clumping them up together—arms with arms, feet with feet, creating an anatomy of appendages. Bolts now boasted as many toes as it took to envelop the metal. Pipes had a hundred elbows. Gauges grew eyes of their own. The entire lower level of the ship evolved into a mosaic of the human form. The evaporator flats went from a murky black to a wave of flesh tones, all within the matter of a month—a patchwork of skin, brown to tan to pale white.

This was my testament to Shelly, emulating her in a sculpture of made-over pipes and gauges. The main evaporator settled for her head, over a hundred lips compiled to form a single pair. Her eyes were eyes within eyes, the irises of others clipped and clustered. Looking into them was to see a hundred glaring back, a hive of sight swarming inside. I convinced myself that the condensation collecting on the pipes was really sweat forming along her body. I had one-upped all the other boys with their worn-down snapshots. My girl was extending herself over the lower deck of the whole ship.

By then, I'd disappeared from the memory of every sailor on board—save for the captain and a few of the higher officers. But they weren't in a position to hear about ghosts on their boat. My body was beginning to adjust to the lack of light. Sleeping through the afternoons left me in the dark for days, the notion of sunlight seeping out from my skin. All that time belowdecks had left me defenseless against its brightness. I couldn't find Shelly on the docks, anywhere. An hour had already gone by with no sign of her. I kept calling home every few minutes. The answering machine picked up each time. Her prerecorded voice talking to me for those few seconds before the machine would beep, beckoning me to talk back. I kept inside the booth, standing apart from the flurry of families grappling for their boys, a dozen hands ushering their children back onto dry land.

I finally phoned for a taxi to take me home.

Heading through the front door of our house, I realized my feet hadn't grown accustomed to the ground yet. My sense of balance was stolen, the seaward sway still ingrained into my muscles. Inside, I shuffled past photographs of Shelly and me, our past sprawling across the walls, each memory reaching out for an empty space—like vines spreading over a bare fence. Shelly had framed our wedding picture since I'd left.

The kitchen was dripping with road maps, the long-since stiffened highways spilling off the table. A puddle of atlases sat solidified below, crumpled up on the floor—the drip off the tabletop collecting over the tiles. When the door closed behind me, the hinges fanned the maps, the large sheets rising slightly off the table.

Shelly was lying on her back, surrounded in her own automotive autopsy. One knee was bent up toward the ceiling, her foot clumsily tucked under her hip. Her other leg was spread out to the far left, a mesh of maps crumpled below her heel. Her arms were raised up over her shoulders. Her hair was tangled in her fingers.

I could picture the moment she slipped in my mind, mapping out the movement of Shelly's hands as they reached back for the counter, hoping to catch her fall, finding nothing but air behind her, loose and watery, the rush of it breezing right through her fingers. I dredged up the instant her skull collided with the tiles, her back arching up. Then flopping down. I couldn't stop looking, unable to convince my eyes to flinch away from her. Her torso was crooked, as if Shelly's spine had tried to flick her pelvis off once she'd hit the floor. Her neck looked like it had attempted to turtle her head down inside her rib cage, her shoulders swallowing up most of her throat. Her chin was tucked in at her chest, the very tip of her face resting on the uppermost segment of her sternum. The *manubrium*. I even knew the name for it, that crater of flesh at the base of her neck. She'd asked me to look it up in the encyclopedia one night, determined to find out what the doctors could call such a beautiful part of the body.

"I have to know," she'd said at my shoulder, kneeling behind me in bed as we scanned through the book's catalogue of medical etchings. "I bet you they named it after one of their wives. That's what I would've done if I discovered the thing. Call it something worthwhile, you know?"

"Here it is," I said, rubbing my index finger over the word. "The manubrium."

"Mana-*what?*"

"Man-u-bri-um. The sterno-cleido mastoid. That's the inter-clavic notch."

"I am not calling that hot part of your bod your *man-*

abreeeum." She'd pulled me down onto the bed, slipping her face into the arch of my neck, nuzzling her mouth over my *manubrium*. She wrapped her lips over the thin rim of bone, sealing those two hollows together.

"I know what I'll call it! Schmupf mf mizzes."

"What?"

"Cup of kisses." She enunciated it perfectly, each word cushioned on a little puff of air. Her chin was ladled by the very vessel.

Now she was on the kitchen floor—her chin resting inside the peak of her sternum, her head overflowing from that tiny bowl of bone. Her clavicles extended upward like bird wings stripped of their feathers, the outspread bones tethered down by her own flesh. Her head was perched over top of that mangled nest of her own body, birdlike—the accident twisting her limbs into a contortionist's roost.

Her skin was blue, her veins blending in with the highways and byways from the surrounding road maps. It looked as if her body had suddenly spread out across the whole floor, her arteries detouring into the atlases' interstates in an extended map of America. Of Shelly. The two had melded into their own country across our kitchen floor.

She could've been dead for weeks. Maybe more. The number of messages on our answering machine attested to her time on the floor. A month of our marriage could have been spent crumpled up right here in the kitchen. The smell had patiently taken to the air, overpowering an old container of potpourri sitting next to the sink. The fresh stink had complete control over the kitchen, lingering in my mouth. My lungs were weighing down with the extra heft of early decay. I felt her enter through my throat. I tried to find fresh oxygen, wading into the vapor as if I was pushing through hip-deep water. I was drowning in my own wife.

There was a notepad on the table. A pencil rest next to it. A few pages had been written on and torn out—some balled up, others stacked on top of each other. I picked one up and started reading.

Will,

Now this is just silly. See what you've got me doing now? You're luring me into writing you a love letter, you lucky bastard—even though I know there's nowhere I can mail it off to. I'd have better luck slipping this note into a bottle and tossing it out to sea than asking the mailman to deliver it to you. The ocean would be full of glass if I'd only have written you a note for every day you've been gone now. You'd hear the sound of bottles knocking against your boat all the time, that slight clink of glass tapping at the hull every day, every night.

The merchant marine should've given you a better address than just the Atlantic. It's not fair, Will—waiting like this. I can't even drop you a line, if I wanted to. What's a girl supposed to do while you're away like this? I'm getting lonely over here. I've received all your postcards—but now I feel cheated. It's unfair that I can't write you back.

Picking up another one, I flattened out its wrinkles and read—

Will,

Know what? After reading your letters over and over again, combing through every one for—oh, over a hundred times, I can hear your voice within the words now. The sound of you lifts off the page. It's almost as if you're here with me, whispering everything you've written right into my ear. I can hear you in your letters. You know that? It's like you're talking to me, saying these sweet things. That's how

good of a writer you are. It doesn't even feel like I'm reading anymore. Just listening to you.

I just wish I could say something back. I'd say hello. Tell you how much I miss you.

Another—

Will,

I know I'm supposed to be patient. You promised me a call in a couple months—but until the phone rings, I've got to find a distraction. Something that's going to calm me down a bit. I can't stop thinking about you. I miss you so much. Enough to do something as silly as this. I've been writing you letters for at least a couple weeks now, trying to put every thought I have of you down on paper. I figured, instead of trying to take my mind off of you—the next best thing to do would be to store those thoughts away. Stash them someplace safe, where I could keep them hidden. I think I've written you over twenty letters already. Maybe more. I don't want to keep count anymore.

And another—

I've become the biggest message in a bottle there is. By the time you come home, you'll know without me even needing to say a single word.

Love,

I lay down next to her, wanting her to wake up. A crackle of maps sounded below our bodies. I curled up at her side, pulling a map over top of us as a blanket. North Carolina covered her chest, her chin pointing toward Winston-Salem. Her eyes kept looking up to the ceiling, lips parted enough to hint at her teeth. The longer I looked at her body, the less the angles looked knotted. The hook in her broken neck shifted into a supple bend. Her warped limbs mellowed into tender interstates, her entire figure flourishing into new roads. I was breathing steadier now, each inhale of my wife settling inside.

I placed my ear over her belly button.

"Can you hear anything?" she'd asked me.

"What am I listening for?"

"I don't know. My tummy grumbling."

"I don't have to put my ear here to hear that."

"What does it sound like?"

Her navel whispered to me, mumbling up how hungry she was. "Want to eat?"

"Is that what it's saying?"

"Rumbles don't lie."

"Jeez. Sold out by my own stomach."

We'd lie in bed, my head resting on her side, listening to this gramophone of flesh playing a steady melody of her pulse. I saw her stomach as a Victrola, where I could slip a different record on and listen to her insides. When she breathed, her belly would swell—the air resonating within that chasm like the bellows of a musical instrument.

"Does it sound like a baby would fit in there?" she asked.

Yes, it did. All I had to do was change the record, put on a new tune.

Got those coolers you wanted, I said. *Just like you asked.*

Spreading out the maps over the floor, I made sure there wasn't a single inch of exposed tile. I laid Shelly out on the table over top of a padding of atlases, remembering the moment I'd carried her into the bedroom after our wedding.

"You take off that tux while I find a way out of this dress."

"No, keep the dress on."

"But I'm returning it tomorrow."

"Take it to the dry cleaners first," I said, starting to hum.

"What's that?"

"Our song."

"We've got a song?"

"Take your pick."

"I want—"

"Hey . . . I said keep the dress on."

"You won't be able to reach me if I keep it on."

"Yeah, I will. Just lay back, okay? Let me do all the work."

"Aye-aye captain."

I straightened out each of her limbs, kneading the rigor mortis free from her joints.

"That feels good."

Humming, the song never broke out of my mouth. I tried evening out as much of her neck as I could without the bone tearing her throat.

"Ooh, right there." Her neck loosened in my hands. "I'll plan our road trip while you're gone—how about that? I'm circling cities we can visit all along the way to Florida. Sound good?"

I stared at my hands, weighed down with her skull.

"You listening to me? Will?"

"Yeah, Shell. Keep going." I looked down to the floor, the roads intersecting at my feet. Every map now served as a diagram for a separate section of her body. I studied our honeymoon trail, tracing the spine of I-95 from Virginia to Florida, discovering a ring of ink crowning a different city in each state. Dunn, North Carolina. Sumter, South Carolina. Brunswick, Georgia. Leading all the way down to Florida. I saw every state line as another bracket to her body, the divide between them corresponding with her limbs. Until there was no telling the two apart. Sifting through the southern states was like scanning over her skin. She had mapped out the entire ride with her body, start to finish.

New mileposts started popping up over the atlases, hundreds of red dots marking new cities that no one had ever heard of or ever lived in before—her blood soaking up the whole country. Shelly's the only map I use now. Those cities have all dried up, browning before my eyes. I've got to make my way to each town before our honeymoon falls apart—which means I've got to find my way out of Virginia. Can you tell me where this road goes? I need to make my way down to Dunn, North Carolina. Ever been there before?

Me, neither.

Suddenly you begin to think of all the things you never got to say. When the moment is gone and all you're left with is every thought you've never shared with someone before, your mind starts searching for a way in which to get that chance back. If the opportunity to talk to a loved one is lost, most people would rather look for the means to say those things than accept their mistake. All those seconds I spent alone, on my own, depending on time to be there for me and Shelly later on—I tallied those moments up, until I was sitting on weeks' worth of squandered ideas, forfeited feelings. I wasn't willing to admit that it was too late. If I wasn't able to get that time back between us, I could at least freeze those unfulfilled emotions—putting her on ice until I could come up with a way in which to tell Shelly everything. It was just a matter of making a pit stop to the closest mini-mart, stocking up on as many bags of ice as these coolers could hold.

The idea of a honeymoon outshined Shelly's accident. This had been our chance at laying our lives down for a while, taking the week off to journey through the country. I could put time on pause, thanks to seven one-gallon bags of crushed ice. Whenever destiny seemed to catch up with us, all I had to do was pull over and pick up another couple of bags—pushing our worries away for as long as Shelly kept refrigerated. No matter how high the temperature went, this highway was littered with enough grocery stores and gas stations to keep these coolers stocked. I'd drain the water out by the side of the road, filling them up with fresh ice, and drive for the next five hours without having to worry over the smell. All we needed were a couple days on the road, anyway. If I could have this honeymoon, I would accept anything that happened before we left. But out here, in this car, time was tossed out the window. Nothing else existed for me. The expanse of this automobile had become all that mattered.

I could never bring myself to sell this car. It's a piece of junk that's cost me enough money just to keep it running. I could've bought a new set of wheels that worked with what I've spent on fixing the transmission alone. Whether it's the engine or a wobbly tire, it's almost as if one part of the car will wreck the second I repair whatever was broken before it. They're taking turns falling apart on me.

Time hasn't been all too kind with my car. This rash of rust has sprouted up around its lower haunches, just around the rear tires. Started eating away at the chassis's underbelly a couple years back. The paint job has gone all raw around the edges, flaking away. What's left is this septic metal, soft enough to fold right in your hand. I should've scrapped this heap years ago. Put it down like some dog too old to even bend its legs anymore—my own Old Yeller on wheels.

But this is my first and only automobile. Never got behind the wheel of another. My mom and dad had surprised me with it when I turned sixteen. Waking up one morning, I looked outside to see this sedan parked out in our driveway. You can imagine what this baby must've looked like back then. The paint job was perfect, not a single blemish on it. I could see my reflection stretching over the hood—my body bending over its chrome, taking to its shape.

Shelly had even left a lock of her hair hanging from the rearview mirror, tied together at both ends. She'd put it there as the ribbon wrapping up my gift—just a red tress, reminding me of her every time I turned on the ignition.

Still there, too. This curl has kept as red as the day she cut it. It's a bit more coarse than it'd used to be, drier than before. But whenever I touch it, rubbing my fingers over the ringlet—I'll feel as if I'm with her, running my hands through her hair as she holds me. She'd lean her head over onto mine, shrouding my body in a canopy of her hair. The two of us would lock eyes inside our new tent. The light from outside would seep through her curls, casting a pink glow over her face.

This was where Shelly and me first lost our virginity. The backseat of this car is as sacred as a temple to me. There's some sentimental value seeped into the upholstery—our sweat soaked into the leather, together. If I press my nose deep enough into the crease back there, I can still smell her. Brings her back every time.

We'd been going steady for a while, somewhere in our senior year of high school. We'd made out in the car before, but sex was something she was saving herself for. I'd figured she'd meant after she got married—but once we were heading home from a flick we'd just gotten out of, Shelly reached her hand over for my leg, her palm saddling right up to my thigh. I hadn't been expecting it—so when I looked down, my eyes leaving the road for a moment, I didn't think to bring them back up again. I just kept staring at her hand, surprised to even see it down there—let alone feel her fingers hooking over my quadriceps.

"Will—"

Tilting my head back up, I felt a warmth of headlights spread over my cheeks. The car had eased into the opposite lane, heading directly into the oncoming traffic. I quickly spun the wheel to the right, bringing us back onto our side of the road—just in time to hear the horn of the other car wailing past.

Shelly hadn't let go, though. Her grip only tightened, squeezing my leg. She had her hand wrapped around the thigh of the leg that had the foot on the gas pedal, connecting each segment to one another. As her fingers dug in deeper, her nails pinching the muscle underneath—I felt my leg extend itself, pressing my foot down onto the pedal. The divider lines on the road began to slip under the car faster than they had before, quickly disappearing below the front fender. We passed a sign saying our speed should've been below thirty-five miles an hour. We were pushing fifty. The arrow kept rising—fifty-two, fifty-five, sixty. The road was easing beneath us so rapidly, I felt my pulse thicken. Shelly felt it, too. Her hand must've been gripping onto an artery down there, my pulse throbbing against her palm.

She was controlling our pace now. The second she let her grip soften around my leg, my foot would swiftly lift off the accelerator. When she'd grab on again, it was like a pinched nerve in my thigh—my entire leg jutting forward, pushing the car even farther down the road. It became a game to her. She'd clasp and release my leg repeatedly, our speed fluctuating up and down. The arrow on the speedometer kept rising and falling, unsure of what direction it was heading in.

None of this was ever said. It all simply happened in silence, the music on the radio the sole sound coming from inside the car. I'd look over at Shelly for a second, watching her follow the road. The dim glow of the dashboard cast this pale blue hue over her face, her skin all watery. If she ever noticed that I was looking at her, all she'd do was smile—her cheeks sealing her eyes shut. She wouldn't look over at me, teasing me by keeping her eyes on the road. At least one of us was, right? I'd simply see her left cheek dimple over. Then I'd feel the muscle in my leg cinch, sending my foot to the floor. I remember hearing the engine seize. The sudden thrust of momentum kicked in, pitching the two of us back against our seats. I alternated between looking out the windshield and over at Shelly, my sight volleying between the two—left and right, back and forth, over and over again. She had started to giggle, her smile widening, lips lifting, eyes slipping even deeper beneath her cheeks. It only got her grip to tighten, my leg beginning to cramp. I couldn't push my foot down any farther. My foot was mashing the gas pedal as if it'd been some bug I wanted to crush, squashing it under the sole of my shoe.

If I could've gotten her to smile any wider, I think I would've forced that pedal through the floor of the car—until my toes scraped over the pavement, until I rubbed my foot right off. I would've done anything to have made her happy just then. There was excitement flushing all over her face, her cheeks darkening the higher we mounted the miles-per-hour. She looked beautiful.

I steered us through the outskirts of town, where the countryside suddenly seeps in, leaving the city way behind. We reached this part of the road that wound around a series of small hills—a wooded area where there weren't any street lamps overhead, no light whatsoever. No stop signs, either. Nothing but trees all around and a bend every half mile. I plowed through those curves, thinking of them as lumps in the pavement that my car could even out.

The tires would scuttle across the asphalt on every turn. I almost lost control of the steering wheel once, taking a bend in the road too fast—sending the rear of the car into a skid, the sedan's hind end sliding over into the opposite lane. The road wasn't even underneath us. We didn't need the pavement anymore. We had picked up enough momentum to lift off the asphalt, the tires spinning through the air. Nothing could keep up with Shelly's grip.

I had my window rolled down, the wind slipping over my left ear. The breeze whipped through, drowning out all the other sounds around us.

Every so often, a pair of pink eyes would catch the headlights—the body of some deer suddenly looming over the side of the road. They'd lift their heads up to us—their limbs stiffening in the ditch as if we'd caught them in the middle of something they shouldn't have been doing, freezing in this fearful stance. After we'd pass, they'd step out into the road—following the flicker of the red taillights through the trees. The brake lights dyed their fur in this bloody color, as if we'd hit the broadside of their bodies—only to disappear as fast as we'd found them. *Poof*—back into blackness.

Keeping her hand on my leg, Shelly reeled the rest of her body toward me—until her chin was perched upon my shoulder. With her lips just inches away from my ear, she whispered, "So where are you taking me, mister?"

"Wherever you want to go."

"Are we there yet?"

"Getting closer."

"Soon?"

"Real soon."

"Good. My hand's hurting."

"I can't even feel my leg anymore. You've cut the circulation off—"

"What?" She couldn't hear me.

"My leg. It's gone."

"Where'd it go?"

We were yelling over the wind now. The air was filling in my left ear, shrill in pitch and constantly shrieking. But on the right, Shelly's breath soothed my mind—her voice easing its way in, settling over the lobe. There was a warmth running down the right side of my neck. It left the other half of my face feeling cool, colder. The air was reckless over there, next to the window. There was a liquid presence to that half of the atmosphere, as if the wind was water filling up the inside of the car. I began to imagine that the car was suddenly sinking. We could've had an accident, where I lost control of the car, driving right into a big body of water, the entire automobile falling to the bottom floor—every crack and valve suddenly flooding with fluid.

It got harder for me to breathe, the air thinning out inside my chest. Even with the breeze barreling over me, I couldn't bring myself to inhale any of it. I was afraid I'd swallow water, instead. In seconds, my head would be submerged. The tide would take over the car, forcing the air out of every corner. My skin was numbing itself, already. Goose bumps were rising up like buoys bobbing over the surface. I would drown inside my own automobile—the car drifting deeper into the depths of this road, settling at the bottom of some unknown ocean.

"Let's pull over." Shelly's breath rushed into my ear again, the warmth of her voice overflowing the lobe and running down my jawbone, my throat. She had breathed into me, resuscitating my senses all over again. The strain on my lungs lessened. I could breathe freely. I felt revived, my vigor returning.

We came upon this clearing. This open field popped up out of nowhere, hedged in with this fence. Shelly let go of me, my leg finally set free for the first time since we'd started speeding. I slammed my foot onto the brakes, rubbing the tires over the pavement. Putting the car in reverse, I pulled back up to the field—finding this stretch of land without any tree in sight. There was nothing out there but empty terrain, open and endless.

There was a gate farther back. I put the car in park, jumping out to open it. The field had a herd of cows out there, somewhere. There wasn't enough light to find them, but I could hear them. They sounded as if they were farther down, farther away from where we were. We didn't go much farther than beyond the fence. Once we passed through the gate, I let the car meander a bit—letting it settle into its own spot—and turned the engine off. There were sounds all around us now. With the car quiet, save for the slight tinkle of metal underneath the hood—everything distilled itself to nature. With the headlights turned off, the dark was everywhere. There was nothing to see, other than the faint trace of the horizon farther down the field. The moon cast its own glow through the windshield, outlining Shelly's body with the slightest trace of light.

You remember those moments. You lock them into your brain for the rest of your life, keeping them close. I could hone in on the glint in Shelly's eye, that slight reflection of light trapped inside. Even the green glow over the right side of her face had an impact on me. She looked aquamarine, her paleness taking in the closest color it could find.

It felt as if we were still underwater, surviving below the surface. The murk of the night was oceanic, thick enough to see nothing other than what was three inches in front of my face. The lightning bugs had become a batch of phosphorescences drifting by, sparking the sky.

Shelly floated over to me, her lips finding my cheek. If she had been aiming for my mouth, she missed by an inch. She kissed her way over, like a mollusk slithering across the ocean floor. When our mouths met, her tongue eased out from the shell of her skull—that snail sliding out from one conch into another. We kissed. We'd become aquatic, slathering ourselves up in a sudden sweat. Our bodies accepted the pressure of the surrounding water. Now we were searching for sustenance through the silt and sand settled at the floor of our own mouths. We kept exchanging breaths, filtering the air through our throats—her exhales becoming my inhales, recycling the same oxygen between the two of us, until our lungs became gummy. We'd become sea slugs of love. Slimy, slippery, suctioning snails. *Romantica aquatica gastropoda.*

We made our way over the headrests and into the rear of the car. The leather was cold, sending a shiver over my back. The seats weren't as worn in as the ones up front, stiffer than what my skin was used to. But Shelly settled herself across the upholstery, resting on her back. It was hard to see all of her just then, the moonlight dim and stilted. What little I saw was this: a part of her shoulder. A sliver of her forehead. Her bottom lip. The tip of her nose would slip in and out of the light, depending on where she turned her head. She'd been wearing this angora sweater, adding an ample amount of fuzziness to her breasts. They looked like sea urchins surging up from the darkness of her chest, their pink tendrils barely lit by the moon.

Her hand reached up for me. I caught a glance of it passing by my face, feeling her fingers wrap around the back of my neck. She reeled me toward her, her palm pressing against my spine until I abided—slowly lowering myself onto her.

There were times when I couldn't tell what part of her I was touching. But whenever my lips strayed away from hers, I simply followed the softness of her skin. At one point I realized I'd been pecking at the upholstery for about a solid thirty seconds. I hadn't caught on until my tongue tasted saltier than before.

"Where are you?" Shelly asked.

"Right here, right here." I quickly buried my face into her shoulder, pecking at the closest bone. Her hands guided me back to her lips, cupping my head within her two palms. The arch of my jaw rested on top of each thumb. She held my head in place, cradling my skull just above hers. We stopped kissing for a second, attempting to stare at each other through the dark. I could hear her breathing—how heavy it had become.

We had to stop at one point so Shelly could pull the seat belt out from under her, the buckle buried into her back. I pressed one hand against the window just above her head, placing both of my feet against the opposite window—allowing myself the leverage to hold my body up enough that I wouldn't crush her. The glass had fogged up, causing my hand to slip. I'd topple onto her every so often. But I'd just shimmy back up, positioning myself above her all over again.

Out of pure frustration, finally tired of fumbling around—I reached up above me and flipped on the car light. The backseat lit up abruptly. We were naked in some places, while our clothes were left clumped up around our legs. Our pants were crammed against the door, still hanging off of our feet. Shelly's bra was tangled around her left arm.

"Turn it off, turn it off!" Shelly squealed, her glance gliding over my head and toward the window.

"What? What?"

Lifting my head, I lost my footing—my heels slipping off the window. I fell on top of her, her knee greeting my groin. Shelly started shrieking, pointing toward the window. I picked myself up, finding myself face-to-face with this cow. The herd had ambled over to the car, surrounding us. They must've been lured over by the sounds we'd been making—peering in through the windows, mooing in retort to Shelly's moans.

"What is it? What is it?"

"It's just a cow."

Shelly ran her arms over her chest, attempting to hide her naked body from the peeping bulls. She exhaled for the first time, the air released with a laugh. "I thought it was some pervert, peeking in."

"We're going to cause a stampede if we don't watch ourselves."

"Really? Think we could?" She smiled. I could just barely see her teeth in the dark.

"Want to try?"

Shelly grabbed hold of me, easing me back down. Now we were having cow-sex. Her lips would loop together, puckering up into an *O*. It was hard to hold back from laughing, the mixture of giggles and moans blending in with one another—*moooooooooooo*.

The drive back home was quiet. Not because we were uncomfortable or didn't know what to say to each other. The moment was there, and we shared it in the silence. Just listening to everything outside again—the wind, the crickets, the cows. Anything that we could get our ears around. The car kept us connected—the impression of Shelly's backside left in the leather, the smell lingering in the air. We rolled up our windows again, breathing it all in. This was us, our bodies. Our first sweat together. We'd made this smell.

I'll be stabbing at the state line by mid-afternoon. North Carolina will welcome me in with a country song playing on the radio, the reception phasing in and out. The dial just barely reaches the stations down here, encrusting the tune with a scab of static. I haven't switched channels since I left home, letting the antenna grab whatever music it can reach—a ligature of white noise connecting these fragments of music together. A sonic Frankenstein. A half hour will go by with nothing but the hack and crackle of the airwaves, the sound resembling the sizzle of burning skin. Even when the antenna can catch a station, the faint hiss of static always underlines the song. I've been conjuring up images of country singers on fire, warbling out their tune in flames. The radio's been letting off a rotten smell, an aroma of slowly smoldering flesh lingering through the car.

Or it could be the coolers. They've been leaking again. I needed to make a pit stop soon, pick up another couple of bags of ice. Shelly's not going to make it to Florida without them.

The divider lines keep crumbling away in front of me. The painted lines break off into a Morse code across the highway. I tried deciphering the mile-long message. I'm able to read a bit of it now, I think.

R-E-D—H-A-I-R—P-A-L-E—G-R-E-E-N—E-Y-E-S—S-H-E-L-L-Y—H-A-S—S-O-M-E—S-P-L-E-N-D-I-D—T-H-I-G-H-S . . .

north carolina

Temperature's set at an all-time record high today, inching closer to those triple digits by the end of the afternoon. Hope everybody's air-conditioning is working out there—because it's only gonna get hotter as the week continues. I tell you, it's times like these that I'm happy to be in here and not in my car. Today's weather has been brought to you by Bill Newman's Used Automo down on Route 7, where you can drive home in your own car the same day you step onto the lot—guaranteed.

tollbooth buddy: wallace reese

Know how many faces filter through my booth a day? I try counting at first, in the morning—but I usually lose track after a half hour. Features all start blending together once my first cup of coffee wears off. From there, it's just a blur of noses. Eyes. Everyone looks the same. For every car passing by, you've got to factor in at least one person behind the wheel. During rush hour, it's usually businessmen. *Mostly* businessmen. They even dress the same. Their foot barely touches the brake when they drive through.

But on the weekends, I get families. There'll be somebody sitting shotgun, a couple of people filling in the backseat. Usually kids.

Kids are the greatest. They're about the only faces I can remember most of the time. 'Cause they're the ones who'll really look. Look at me. Adults never do that. Sometimes, I'll get a little girl pressing her face against the window so hard, it'll lift the tip of her nose up to her eyes—until I'm looking right down her nostrils. Fitting her lips over the glass, she'll blow—her cheeks bulging out so much, her face balloons right up. Her mouth will open just enough that I can almost hear her teeth tapping against the glass, her tongue squished in between. Makes her look like one of those fish you see at the pet shops, sucking the algae off their aquarium. When she exhales, there's that perfect circle of fog inside her mouth. If the girl's fast enough, she can spell out a word with her breath before her parents drive away. They use their fingers to write me a message. Some'll say "hi" to me. Others try spelling out their names. Usually, they can only scribble the first two or three letters—leaving me with a "Ka" or a "Sar" and that's about it.

But a face like that's easy to remember. Cheeks all red from blushing. A missing tooth or two. A little smudge of grease on the glass from where she stuck her nose against the window. I'll hold on to a face like that for the rest of the day, no problem.

It's their parents who won't notice me. Most I'll ever get from them is a passing glance as they hand me a dollar, a second's worth of sight slipping in between us when I give them back their change.

The worst is when there's that tiny bit of contact between our fingers. That can be a little embarrassing. I've had women drop their change, just because I accidentally touched them, thinking I'm either making a pass or trying to pull them out of their own car. Then it's *my* job to get out from the booth and pick up the coins *they* let slip through *their* fingers. Hunker down on the road and reach under *their* car, blindly patting at the pavement for *their* quarters—wherever they rolled off to. Hoping they're not stuck under a tire. I broke a finger once when this lady decided she didn't want her change anymore—putting her foot on the gas pedal before I could move my hand out from under her tire. I had an imprint of George Washington's face on the tip of my finger for a whole week—while on the other side, I had the ridges of her Michelin wrapping around my knuckles.

It'd just be nice for someone to leave a lasting impression on me, for once. That's all I'm asking for. Hundreds of people pass me by every day, and I can barely remember a single face by the time I clock out. Only thing I take home is a head full of phlegm, this film of exhaust coating my throat. I'll be coughing up smut for about the first hour I'm off. I have to drink a gallon's worth of water just to loosen up my windpipe. Wash the day away—get me breathing freely again. Not so choked, where every inhale sounds like someone's muffler backfiring. Never had a job that gave me respiratory problems before—but here I am, rasping away. I'm stashing an old jelly jar in my bathroom, another one in the kitchen. I've got one more next to my bed. Whenever I cough up a mouthful of motor oil, I'll spit—keeping it until I've got enough phlegm to march right into my boss's office, drop a jar on his desk, and demand he pay my doctor bills. I need to get some workmen's comp for all this—'cause nowadays, I need to lather up my gullet just to keep from losing my voice. I've been bringing a milk jug filled up with tap water with me to work. I leave it at my feet in the booth, taking a swig every so often—just so there won't be as much soot crusting up my esophagus by the end of the day.

All that water ever does for me, though, is drag my bladder down. I need to pee before my first break, *hours* before—stranding me in the middle of this turnpike with nowhere to go. And I mean *go*. Now I have to bring another jug with me to work, an empty one—relieving myself with one hand, taking people's toll money with the other. Hoping no one notices that I have my pants down in here.

Sure it can be a lonely job. Not because there's nobody

around, but because *everybody's* around. Sometimes, there are too many people, you know? Look at all that asphalt out there. Nothing but turnpike, as far as I can see. I go through days when the traffic's backed up so much, I can't even see the road. The lanes just aren't there, anymore. The highway will be all gone. Just rows and rows of cars clumping bumper to bumper. People forget all about the divider lines the closer they budge forward, tangling into each other—herding their way up to me. They honk their horns so loud, sometimes I can barely even hear myself think. It's a stampede. Everybody's always in such a rush, needing to get to wherever they're going, *fast*. Once they've tossed in their fifty cents, their foot's off the brake and right back on the gas pedal—leaving me with a lung full.

That's why I remember this guy so well. He lingered for a while. He wasn't in such a hurry to head off, actually sticking around. Put his car in park and just started talking to me. Said his name was Will. Will Colby. I'm looking at all the automobiles lining up behind him, honking their horns—but that didn't faze the man one bit. He just kept chatting away, talking on about how he'd never driven to Florida before.

What's in Florida? I ask—figuring, what could a little conversation hurt? Didn't matter to me whether or not he parked his car in front of my booth. I wasn't going anywhere. Let those other cars move over into another lane, if they were in such a hurry.

My honeymoon, he says.

Honeymoon? I ask, glancing over to the empty seat next to him. *Don't you need a wife to go on one of those?*

Only when you want the marriage to last, he said, which got me chuckling.

Nothing struck me as being too odd about him. He wasn't doing anyone any harm, sitting there. I actually appreciated it. Seemed like a fitting *fuck you* to everybody else on the road, which made it fun for me. I saw the wedding band on his hand, so I knew he wasn't lying about his wife—wherever she was. Wasn't any of my business, so I didn't ask. The road can be lonely, especially when you're traveling across the country. I'm surprised more people don't take the opportunity to say *hey* to us toll folks. It's not as if we're machines or anything. When the sign says there's an *operator on duty*, you're assured some flesh and blood along this highway. We're good for more than just a receipt.

First time I felt like this job was taking its toll on me was when I thought I was seeing the same face, over and over again. Had this family drive through in their station wagon one weekend, their little girl in the backseat. She looked familiar to me. There was this gap in her teeth, a few missing up front. She pressed her face against the glass, her nose drifting up enough to pry her lips apart, opening her mouth just a bit for me to see inside. The window frosted over fast—that black cavern between her cheeks disappearing in one breath. I could've sworn I'd been stuck in that fog before. But this girl was gone before I could even blink, her father tossing in his fifty cents and driving away. About four hours and a hundred faces later, I found hers all over again. That girl's lips were wriggling against the window, right in front of me. I think I'm seeing things—so I let them go through my booth without saying a word. But sure enough, later on that same day . . . she's sitting in the backseat of a Buick now—staring at me, giving me that funny face. The cars changed, the parents changed. She's the only thing that kept constant. Her freckles, the color of her hair. Pressing her face up against the window, her cheeks spread over the glass, her nose leaning to the side, its cartilage tender enough to fold in half. She puckered up her lips and blew, the rush of air forcing her mouth open into a perfect *O*—the window thickening into a glass of milk that I wanted to drink from. When she ran out of air, she leaned back into her seat, an imprint of grease and breath left on the window—like a ghost still staring me down, its mouth hollow and eyes all gone. This girl was looking at me through the screen her lungs had made, a fading mask over her own face, the residue of her mouth melting off the glass until I could see her clearly again.

Do you know what the universal sign for *roll down your window* is? Take your hand and ball it up into a fist. Lift your fist up to about your shoulder. And just start churning. Just like this. Like the gears on a train, lead with your fist and rotate. Draw a circle in the air with your knuckles. Punch first, then bring back your elbow. Round and round. *Choo-choo.*

Give that sign to a girl sitting in the backseat of her parents' car, and maybe three times out of ten, she'll do it. She might even say *hi*.

If she does, I'll usually say something like, *Where you going?*

And she'll usually say something like, *The beach*.

And then I'll usually say something like, *Mind if I come along?*

The whole family's speeding off before the girl can even answer.

Where would you go, if you had the chance? this Will Colby asked.

Hadn't given it much thought, really. It's funny—I've had the itch to head out for as long as I started working here, but I can't put a finger on any place I'd like to go. When you've been stuck in this booth for as long as I have, you forget what's out there. Guess I got used to the idea of everyone else heading off somewhere, while I just stayed behind. *Florida, maybe? What have they got down there?*

I'll let you know on my way back—how about that?

Sounds good to me. I'll make sure to switch shifts with someone on the other side of the highway.

Give me a week and I'll be back . . .

I wouldn't say I was holding my breath for the man, but I did switch to the northbound lane a couple days ago. Just in case. Never know what might happen out here, you know? He could be driving through any day now. When he did, I'd ask him what it's like down there, how was his honeymoon. At least it breaks up the monotony a bit, sitting here. He gave me something to look forward to.

Two more hours and I'm off. The homestretch is the toughest time to get through. It's hard to stay awake sometimes, sitting in this sardine can all day. I'll start dozing off in the afternoon, when traffic's slow. When the tolls are supposed to switch over from *operator on duty* to *exact change only*, I'll wake up and it's suddenly rush hour—the cars lining up for miles.

There's a reason for this toll. I'm what separates you from where you are and where you're going. Without me, you could be anywhere. You'd be lost.

It was just nice to have someone to talk to for a change.

william colby

The air conditioner is exhausted by now, all the hours of pumping cool breeze finally fatiguing the machine—reducing it to filtering the hot air from outside. Having that mugginess blow through the vents is like leaning in toward someone's mouth, the exhale slipping past their teeth. Septic breath. Smells like oil burning. Rotten rubber. Whatever's in this engine's stomach, the odor of it is trailing through—stinking up the car. I've had to roll my window down, just to get a fresh breath.

Here was our honeymoon, decaying away. You make this venture only once in your life, a pilgrimage of love. Where that road takes you is beyond this earth, love lifting you up off the ground. Florida was just one long launching pad—a state so slender, all we needed to do was barrel straight down, gunning it all the way until we reached the ocean. And from there—*up, up, and away.* Instead of a trail of tin cans clattering off the rear bumper, me and Shelly had a collection of coolers gathered in the backseat.

Crossing through North Carolina, I started finding signs at the side of the road. They were posted on broom handles, poking out of the ground. In white paint, the first one read *Pull*. Nothing else. The letters had dripped off the board before the paint even had a chance to dry. The *L*s just ran right off the sign. About a quarter of a mile down, there was another—this one reading *On Over*. The next, *For Your*. Next, *Fresh Fruit*. Finally, *And Veggies*. It took over a mile just to find out what we were coming up to, this fruit stand settled in at the side of the road. It was a shack barely holding itself up—a row of wooden planks standing on end, braced together by a couple of two-by-fours. Enough automobiles had whizzed by to nearly push it over—the constant current of cars causing a torrent of wind to blow on the stand's broadside, leaving the whole hut in this permanent leaning position. Driving by at sixty miles an hour, it looked as if the stand was just about to topple over on itself.

As I passed it, I glanced over. Inside, there were two faces surrounded by piles of green—a man and a child sitting next to each other. The boy's head turned with my car, following me down the road—while the older man kept his neck still, staring straight ahead.

The wheel was turning toward the right before I even put my foot on the brakes. I pulled over so fast, the tires spat up gravel—a loud tinker of pebbles striking the chassis's underbelly.

From the rearview mirror, I saw the boy running out from the fruit stand. He was waving his arm up in the air at me, hailing me. His reflection swelled up within the mirror. The closer the kid got to the car, the more yellow his arm looked, all stiff and ribbed. Now it seemed scaly. Almost kerneled. Took me to squint to notice he didn't have any fingers—just a slender staff swinging over his head. He rushed up toward the window at my left, knocking on the glass with this stump of yellowed bone. This kid had somehow strapped a shucked ear of corn to his elbow, positioned exactly where the rest of his arm should've been. It was tethered to his elbow with the husk—actually wrapped around and roped off, so that the corn and upper half of his arm were bound together. He never broke his smile, waving his vegetable appendage—so eager for me to wave back. And when I did—too stunned to do otherwise—his smile only went wider, this feeling of achievement rushing over his cheeks. Must've been happy enough for someone to have stopped, even happier that someone was acknowledging him. The number of cars he counted passing by probably reached up into the hundreds every day—while he could add the number of people that actually pulled off to the side of the road with one hand. Which was for the better.

"Don't mind the arm, now." His father explained, "He puts that cob on and thinks no one's gonna notice what's missing. We've gotten so used to it that I forget to mention to him to take it off around strangers."

"I don't mind."

"He's frightened off some customers before—so we just need to take better notice to who pulls over, I guess."

"Mind me asking what happened?"

"Genetics gets credit, prodded along with a little bit of phosphates and surfactants. See, I used to be the foreman at the Pratt Chemical Processing Plant, mixing toxic cocktails for pesticide companies right alongside the Goldsboro River. I hadn't admitted as much to my wife at the time, but I'd been dumping about a thousand gallons of waste into the water every day. Never worried once over the occupational hazards of my job. My conscience was clean of contamination—up until an entire school of trout washed up onto the shore, sporting more eyes than their skull should've had sockets for. The local newspaper made a fuss over it for weeks. The front page always displayed a full-color photo of a five-eyed, open-mouthed trout staring right at the camera—its body held up in the air by the hands of some local fisherman trying to lean into the picture. If you turned to the center page, more than likely, you'd find a centerfold of one of those fish lying along the shore—like it was posing for some *Playboy* pictorial, looking all seductive by spreading itself out on the sand. One of its bedroom eyes would always be winking at you, seeming to say, *How's about you and me take a dip, mister? I won't bite.*

"Since there wasn't much else going on in Dunn, news coverage didn't die down for months. Every fisherman from here to Pinehurst was suddenly complaining to the papers about how they'd caught a couple croakers with an extra pair of tail fins. It was my responsibility to deny any possibility of the plant polluting the river, my face making it to the front page of the newspaper almost every day—my picture placed right next to one of those mutated mackerels. The photo would always have me in mid-sentence, my mouth as wide open as the fish printed next to me. At times, it was hard to tell just who was who.

"If you scroll through the lead article printed in Tuesday, June 6, 1983's late edition of the *Goldsboro Nugget*, you can find myself quoted as saying, 'For my family, and the family of every employee here in this plant, I promise you—we are not putting this river at risk. Or the fish, or the people who swim in it.' And not one month later, I was tendering my resignation—quitting the very day Elridge here was born. The moment the doctor held him up to me, his skin looking all oily and placental—I suddenly wondered where the rest of his left arm was. I couldn't tell if he was reaching up to his mom or not, because below his elbow just tapered off into a dull point—like a candy-cane licked down to nothing, a nub of flesh sucked off to the bone.

"And Elridge wasn't the only one. For the next few months, every baby born from a Pratt employee had complications. If you were on the plant's payroll, chances were your fecundity had become contaminated. Mothers were flushing a storm of deformities out from their wombs all over town."

"Doesn't that make the soil around here a little dangerous?"

"Ah, hell. Most folks won't grow a thing in the ground now, anyhow. The water's still contaminated, spoiling the soil. But that didn't stop me from setting up this stand. I sell vegetables to tourists now. Contorted gourds, misproportioned potatoes. You name it, we grow it.

"Elridge helped me build this stand. I duct-taped a hammer to his nub and slipped some nails into his mouth while I held the boards up for him to pound in place. We spend the afternoons here on the highway—watching cars pass by, waiting for someone to pull over. When sales are slow, I'll strap this corn cob onto his arm and we'll step out into the road. I'll pitch a cabbage head his way, helping him practice his swing. Elridge wants to grow up to become a baseball player. Pitch for the Mariners. Every night, before his head hits the pillow, his right hand finds its way around the stump of his left, his fingers wrapping over the smooth nub like most kids grip a baseball. *Dear God, please give me an extra inch in my arm tonight—so that I can grow up to become the best pitcher this town has ever seen. I promise I'll hit a homer in your honor, if you just help me out.*

"And every morning, he'll wake up and pull out his ruler, measuring his arm to see if it grew any overnight. But that nub never breaks the three-inch mark. He'll never make it to the major leagues without an extra six inches."

He continued to talk on about a bunch of old Pratt employees getting together to have a company picnic, for old times' sake. Bring all the families back together for a barbecue or something. A bunch of mothers set up some card tables in the plant's old parking lot. By now, the pavement was supposedly all cracked and overrun with weird-looking weeds—but with a few balloons and a couple streamers, it felt as if the building was having a grand reopening. Looked good as new, as far as he was concerned. The day's big event wasn't the fruit salad, though. What really marked the occasion was the induction of Dunn's first deformed Little League baseball team. Elridge's father had decided to coach the kids in some friendly competition, trying to boost up their morale with some sports.

"Before they hit the field, I got the team to huddle up for a pep talk. I told them it wasn't about winning the game, but doing the best they could. I didn't want them to think of their handicaps as a hindrance—but as a special power. Something that made them unique, that no one could take away. Like they were superheroes. Each one of them had his own little gift.

" 'Even if you lose today,' I said, 'you'll all be winners to me.' "

"How was the game?"

"We lost." The way the man said it made me feel like the conversation was over. "He manages well enough without it." He mussed up Elridge's hair. The boy brought the cob up to his head, trying to push his dad's hand away.

A car passed by the three of us driving so fast the wind nearly blew me back a step. The air itself tightened, dragged along with the car—sounding out in this loud whip of wind. I seemed to be the only one affected by it, wincing under the intensity. They must've gone deaf to traffic by then.

The man pulled up an apple from the pile. "Here, pitch him with this. He's such a prodigy at the plate, he can hit just about anything." I didn't expect him to throw it, flinching from the polished red heading toward me. The apple passed by my chest and fell onto the road, rolling across the highway. The boy went running for it, scurrying over the pavement.

"Elridge! Elridge!" The man kept calling. "Get out of the road for Christ's . . ."

Before he could finish, a car sped by. It came out of nowhere—missing Elridge by inches, running over that apple. Its red skin split under the tire, a gush of white mush spreading over the asphalt. Elridge's body turned with the car—his weight so light, the current of wind must've reeled him along, spinning him around.

"What did I tell you, son? Never head out onto the highway unless you look both ways!"

The boy came running back, clutching the cob to his chest. The father rested his hand on Elridge's head. His fingers spread down the boy's temples, his palm nearly covering his entire scalp like a baseball cap.

Elridge stood on one side of the road, while I crossed to the other. Home plate was nothing but a leaf of lettuce spread over the asphalt. He scraped his heel across the pavement, struck his rump with the end of his corn cob, shaking out the dust settling into its kernels. Even from across those two lanes, I could see his eyes tighten—squinting at me to see what I'd pitch.

"Hit a homer, son!" Elridge's father sat back in the shade of the fruit stand, umpiring the entire event from inside the cool air. He was coach, catcher, and fan in the stand—all in one.

Elridge nodded at me, as if to say he was ready. He looked serious now, different from before. His face changed, ready to bat this apple into the outfield—which there was plenty of. There was nothing for miles out here but empty fields.

My first pitch was a clumsy one. I lobbed the apple into the air underhanded, its redness striking the sun. It didn't even reach across the road. The apple struck the highway and rolled to the boy's feet.

"You're gonna have to pitch harder than that!" Elridge's father shouted out.

The boy picked the apple up and tossed it back to me. The apple was bruised now, about an inch of its skin dented inward. Its red flesh was sinking in, the fruit soft and bleeding juice.

This time, I swung my arm around a couple times—only to toss the ball up a little too high. This pitch didn't look as if it was going to make it over the plate. We all watched the apple spin through the air, going up higher, higher, its shape dwindling down to a simple red dot—then bigger again, larger, redder, closer. Elridge slipped into his hitting position—one foot back, the other on the plate. His elbow bent, he brought the cob up close to his shoulder. I don't think his eyes ever left the apple. When the fruit fell in front of his face, the air cracked itself open. In a single swing, the apple's skin broke, juice bursting everywhere. Before I could catch a fragment, Elridge was looking both ways, seeing that the highway was clear. He ran to the divider lines, hopping onto first base, then continuing toward second. He was heading for third before I could even figure out where the apple was—in the air, on the road, rolling through the fields. The largest chunk was resting in the ditch. The apple's skin split open, shreds flapping in the wind. I bent over to pick it up, hearing Elridge's father holler, "Head for home, son! You got it! You got it!"

By the time I had the apple in my hand, Elridge was sliding over home plate—his foot pushing the sliver of lettuce off the road. I threw the apple at him, anyways—thinking there'd be a catcher waiting for it, ready to strike him out. The scraps of apple just disintegrated into the air, spreading across the highway in red and white dollops.

His father stood up, clapping and cheering. "A run for the home team! One to nothing!"

We had gone through about five apples before I finally felt like I was getting somewhere with the game, holding my own. Elridge's father gave up on watching, dozing off in the shade.

The apple kept shuttling back and forth between us. I had gripped its polished skin so much, the pulp underneath had begun to soften. When the apple made its way to Elridge's hand, he kept it—choosing to finally bite into it instead of tossing it back to me. Lord knows what toxins were in his mouth right now, slipping down in that swallow.

The afternoon was wearing down, the sun beginning to set. I needed to get back on the road before it got too late, realizing how far away I was from hitting Florida.

"You still want some fruit?"

"Sure."

I took as much as Elridge was willing to give, making sure not to wake his father. I filled up the front seat with enough peaches and apples and tomatoes to ripen the air inside the car, softening up the smell from behind me.

"Can I give you something, Elridge? A gift between you and me?"

"Sure."

Handing him a cooler that contained Shelly's left arm, I knew Elridge would never pine over those missing six inches again. It seemed fitting—no matter how out of balance the two limbs would look when he duct-taped them together. Like putting two puzzle pieces in place, Elridge could fasten the raw end of her arm onto his stub. It would be like a fresh sapling springing up from an old stump.

Shelly was beginning to regenerate herself, I thought. She was sprouting out from the South already, the bits of her body taking root within the people I met on our honeymoon. I was filling in for Johnny Appleseed without even realizing it, suddenly beginning to believe I had enough limbs to cultivate a crop along every pit stop.

We've passed by so many photo opportunities along the road. Driving through Goldsboro, there was this turnoff for tourists to take pictures of the scenery. There were bathrooms for those who needed it, snack machines for people who were hungry—along with an open deck overlooking the neighboring Goldsboro River. The tangle of tourists was unbelievable, almost every state represented judging by their license plates. Folks as far as California had come here, snapping off a photo of the family alongside the highway.

When I want to remember a moment, try to freeze a piece of time between me and Shelly—instead of snapping off a photo, it seems smarter to leave something of ours where we want that memory to stay. Rather than taking something away, it's better to leave something behind. That way, wherever we are, a piece of us will always be there. Shelly could grow back to me. I'll sift through the South, spreading seeds all across the countryside. Whenever I look over my shoulder, back toward where I've been—I'll find her sprouting out behind me. There'll be life within my wake. This is the most fertile soil there is. With all the pictures of her in my wallet (there's more pictures of my wife in there than money by now), I'll stick one over wherever I've buried her. It reminds me of an empty seed packet poking out from someone's garden, marking what's been planted.

Here's Shelly. Water regularly and she should sprout out soon enough.

south carolina

For those of you who are just tuning in, I'd like you to know—it's not too late to save your soul. There's a storm cloud forming over our heads, people—and it's taking the shape of Satan this very second. Look out your windshields, people. I want you to think back to those moments when you were a little kid, staring up into the skies—imagining a white rabbit hopping through the heavens or a teddy bear floating over your head. Those clouds could've conjured up an ice cream cone for you, just waiting to get licked. But brethren—if you can see the cloud that I'm talking about now, just outside your car, all black and thunderous, I want you to imagine what it could be. What form will it take, people? Why, it's shaping up to be the Devil himself. Look at the horns sprouting out from its head. See the lightning in its eyes. Don't be fooled by Mother Nature now, people—the end of days is upon us. We've fed this beast with the exhaust from our own automobiles—and now he's fit to walk the land, once again.

tollbooth buddy: audrey dow

My mother kept telling me that it wasn't so smart to take this job, inhaling the air that I do. *You're breathing for two now,* she'd say. *Working this tollbooth isn't safe for your baby.*

Exhaust pipes never frightened me, though. I've been smoking my mother's cigarettes ever since I was twelve years old, palming a few Capris from her purse when she wasn't looking. My lungs still feel sturdier than a burlap bag. Not like these cars are gonna get me any closer to cancer. My phlegm was yellow before I was even sucking down this soot.

But then I'd start thinking about Josey, curled up right here in this booth with me. *In* me. Thought about her lungs—pinker than the inside of my lip, small enough to rest right on my tongue. Figured they looked like a pair of butterfly wings, developing in her chest. I imagined her first breath fluttering through her rib cage, her lungs swelling up and sinking. Her heart could've just flapped away from me.

Thought about how these fumes could've been harming her before she even got a chance to breathe for herself. That I was choking my child—just by trying to earn enough money to take care of her on my own. But this job pays better than my last, so I can't quite see myself quitting it just yet. Manning that cash register at our local grocery store wasn't much different than squatting in this tollbooth all day, anyway. Both had me at the helm of more faces than I could ever remember, all of my customers blurring together. All those grocery shoppers would hand me their money without even looking at who they were giving it to and I'd bag their food—while these businessmen in their cars just toss me their fifty cents. Not much difference between the two, as far as I can tell.

But out here, I'm earning an extra dollar for every hour I work. I don't even have to worry over a paper cut from those shopping bags. Never have to heft a load of groceries out to some elderly woman's car, only for her to forget where she parked the damn thing in the first place. Here, I just sit and give people their change. Worst I ever had to deal with out here was some bum thinking he could make a pass at me. I guess they just couldn't see my belly from that far down, looking up at me from their car. I've gotten everything from a flick of the tongue to truckers' phone numbers—but whatever. I've got ten seconds to reckon with and that's all. They're on their way before I can even remember what they looked like. Bring on the next car.

You better believe that beat the grocery store. No cracked eggs, no crushed containers of yogurt. Just a little cough from all this exhaust and that's about the worst of it. I can even listen to my portable radio out here. Sing along, if I want to. I'll spend most of the day just watching the traffic go by—thinking to myself that all these cars are nothing more than ripples in a stream, trickling their way into my booth like I'm some dam they have to pass through. This here highway is nothing but a river of automobiles. I've got water all around me, everywhere. When Josey's old enough to ask me just what it is that her mother does for a living, well—you better believe I'm going to tell her that I'm an artery funneling the flow, making sure traffic doesn't clot up on the road.

Sounds more special when I say it that way. Makes this job more interesting than it really is.

That'll make her proud of me.

Hell, I'll even tell her how I named her. Saw it on someone's license plate, passing through my booth. It was one of those personalized plates, coming up from South Carolina—J-O-S-E-Y, the letters all wrapped in magnolia. *Josey*. I read it just once and couldn't stop myself from thinking about how beautiful it sounded. When I said it to myself out loud, I swear—the second that word was in my mouth, my throat putting a little voice behind that name—there came this kick from within me. I'm not lying. Now I'm not so sure what kind of sign most folks need to know what sex to expect from their child before they're born, but saying that name got my baby to bunt the backside of my belly so hard, I just knew. That was enough for me. I named her before I even knew for sure she was going to be a girl. Never had myself one of those sonograms. Didn't need to see some shadow on a television screen to believe it. I just knew. I could feel her inside myself just fine.

Josey. Breathing the air in right along with me.

Her father? Your guess is as good as mine. Probably better, even. There's this one guy—*Patch*. Used to be one of the bag boys working down at the grocery store. We'd take our smoke breaks in the back alley together. The manager wanted us to hide our vice, hoping to give the store some *family* appeal, which was funny to me, having Patch bag groceries for these grandmothers and all.

With his eagle tattoo and his dangling dagger earrings, I don't even think Patch's family would've laid claim to him. He never talked about his parents to me, at least. I'd mouth off about my mother all the time, but he never . . . uh, reciprocated. Never said a word about himself at all, really. Closest I ever came to knowing what was on his mind was when he slipped his hand onto my thigh. Not that I brushed him off or anything. I mean, I didn't tell him to let go.

One day, rather than have a cigarette the two of us took our fifteen minutes and snuck inside the meat locker behind the deli. I'd never been back there before. Took one look at those racks of ribs hanging from the ceiling and nearly passed out—this slight swing rocking the beef back and forth on their hooks, looking like those cows had all grown wings or something. They all just opened up their chests and tried to fly away. It was enough to make me go vegetarian, never eat another mouthful of meat ever again. I swear.

Patch dead-bolted the freezer door while I spread out a couple pairs of those starched white butcher aprons over a pile of tenderloins. Didn't want to stain my skirt, you know? It'd leave me smelling like some slaughterhouse slut for the rest of the day. We lay down together, in the cold. Patch put his arm around my shoulder to warm me, the two of us talking to each other. I'm telling him about how I'm still living with my mother, trying to earn up enough money to get my own place, talking on and on about my life—when suddenly his other arm comes around my shoulder, cinching me against his chest. He leans over on top of me, forcing me down—my back stiffening up from the frozen meat beneath my shoulder blades. And he starts kissing me. Our name tags kept tangling up. Finally, mine just ripped right off my shirt. Left this tear down the front, just below the collar—which was going to be a tough one to explain to my manager. That was my best work shirt. Only work shirt I had, really.

My thighs were pretty much numb by the time he slipped himself in. All I could see were our exhales spreading out from our mouths, fogging over—our breath weaving into each other.

The two of us just lost track of time. Fifteen minutes stretched out into thirty, maybe more. Neither of us knew what time it was until someone's fist started banging on the other side of the freezer. Patch probably would've leapt up if his lower back hadn't been frozen to the floor. I swear, we'd thawed an imprint of his ass into the broadside of that tenderloin. His rump raised the temperature enough to melt its way into the meat.

My cheeks were so frostbitten, they stung. Felt like there wasn't any circulation slipping through my legs. Couldn't feel anything below my belly button.

When Patch finally opened the door, Mr. Etna, our manager, was standing there next to the deli man—both of them looking at us as if they knew exactly what'd been going on. Don't ask me how. They could smell it, see it. Lord only knows. They just knew somehow. It was like we had left the microphone on at one of the cash registers, broadcasting our smoke break through the entire store.

We were fired on the spot. Both of us. Didn't even get the chance to clock out. Lost a day's wage getting laid in the deli locker.

A month later I found out I'm pregnant. My mother makes me tell Patch he's going to be a father. Only way she's going to let me stay in my own house is if I get him to pay child support. So I go over to his place, knock on his front door. He won't even let me inside. He just stands behind the screen, leaning there—looking at me as if it were *my* fault for *him* getting fired. So I tell him. I just cup my belly and say he left something of his inside me—and he simply slams the door, right in my face. Felt like he slapped me, he shut it so hard. I didn't even think about walking away, I was so stunned. Just stood there, staring at the door. Only thing that woke me up was hearing him yelling at me from inside, hollering for me to get off his property.

I did. Walked away bawling. Don't ask me why. Wasn't like he meant much to me.

But, you know. Slamming the door in my face kind of fucked up my chances for child support.

So Patch packs up and leaves town, okay? Know how I found that out? Get this—this boy's dumb enough to drive through my tollbooth on the second day of my new job. He's got to give *me* his fifty cents so that *I'd* let him pass. I mean, can you imagine the odds of that happening? It was astronomical. Felt like fate was giving me a chance to settle the score. Destiny had ordained me one more moment to get even with the prick.

Well, what do you think I did? Kept dropping his toll money, that's what. He'd hand me his fifty cents and for some reason, the quarters kept slipping right through my fingers—like they were greasy or something. All oiled up from his hand. We spent ten minutes doing this—him opening his car door, picking up his change, giving it back to me, only for the money to fall through my fingers all over again. Patch got so fed up, he just gunned the gas and sped through. Left me with a little *fuck you* under his breath before peeling off. Some highway patrolman pulled him over a few miles down, fining him fifty dollars for trying to cheat me out of my toll.

That's what he gets. That's the least of what he deserves. That fifty cents was the closest thing to him paying me child support that I'll ever get. I even kept his two quarters, leaving them on my bedside table at home.

I tell you, watching all these businessmen drive through here every day gets me thinking about a proper father. For Josey, I mean. You should see these men. Some of them are looking pretty handsome, if you ask me. Clean-shaven, nice car. Suit and a tie. No wrinkles as far as I can tell. I wonder what they see when they look at me. If they even notice that I'm here. When I could spot one of these men in my lane, getting closer to my booth, I'd lean over, so that my belly wasn't showing so much. Sometimes, I'd even sink into my booth a bit, so that my breasts would be just at the window—everything below that hidden behind the door. Smiling, I'd greet them with a *good morning*. Maybe even ask them how they're doing. I figure, I've got about five seconds to sell myself, so I try spending it wisely. I check their ring finger when they hand me their money, seeing if there's an emptiness in between their knuckles—that space saved for me. If I can't find a wedding band, I try smiling wider. Ask them where they're off to. What's their hurry.

It's wishful thinking, I know. But I have to pass the time somehow, right? I'm just waiting for my knight in shining armor to drive up to me, roll down his window, and whisk me out of this booth.

Figured I'd found him. Hadn't happened the way I'd imagined it, exactly, but this man sure did sweep me off my feet. You see, Josey decided to make her way into the world while I was sitting right here. I was handing this trucker his receipt when my water broke, spilling all over the floor. My eyes just widened, without a clue as to what I should do. Looking out onto the highway, I saw all these cars lining up in my lane—families, businessmen, buses—and hoped that there'd be a doctor driving up soon. Maybe even an ambulance that could take me away. But all I saw were minivans, station wagons. I could feel my insides shift, as if my intestines were tightening up. There was this heave in my belly, my stomach lunging for the floor. I leaned over, catching myself on the register realizing that there was barely enough room for me to even kneel down. I couldn't reach the floor if I wanted to. Had to simply stand there, hunched over, holding on to my belly as if it were going to fall right off.

The whole time, I'm hearing this clatter of coins clinking all around me—all these people passing through my booth, paying me no mind. The floor's getting red, my legs all wet, and the only thing I can think of doing is just to take my hand and try stopping Josey from diving out of me. I gripped onto myself and held on, praying for her to wait until my shift was over. I had a little under an hour before I could clock out—pinching my hips, taking in deep breaths. Giving people their change.

My head was starting to spin, this dizziness slipping in, until I couldn't focus on the money in my hand. I was probably giving people back their quarters, letting them ride off with more money than they had given me to begin with. I swear, I thought I was going to faint . . . until this one man asks me, "You feeling all right, ma'am?"

He's sitting behind the wheel of his station wagon, his arm outstretched toward me, holding a dollar. I reach for it, accidentally using the hand that I've had in my pants, and grab that dollar with some bloody fingers. This man, I swear. His eyes just widened. Must've thought I'd hurt myself or something. He puts his car in park, rolling down his window to the hilt. Leaning out toward me, he's asking me what's wrong—but all I can really hear are the horns suddenly blaring all around us. They're making such a racket, I'm getting a headache. He's slipped out of his car, pulling himself up to me. Thought he was going to try to jump in my booth. He takes one good look at me—holding Josey back from breaking through, the floor so slippery that I can barely stand up. His face went whiter than a bleached bedsheet. Looked like one of those presidents on a coin—his complexion all silvery and pale. That's when I screamed. The pain had been building up so much, I couldn't hold back anymore. There were enough car horns honking all around us that it seemed safe to just yell. Just let it all out. Finally. This man, he tries to pick me up. Get me into his car, I guess. But that's not happening. He hoists me up from my shoulders, lifting me off the floor by about an inch or so—only to let go, my weight too much for him. He tried again, but I wasn't going anywhere. It's hurting *so much*. My thighs are on fire. Felt just like those racks of beef back at the deli locker, my hips all pried apart and hanging wide open. This man's telling me to breathe, acting as if he's my Lamaze partner or something—asking me to push, begging for me to squeeze. Half of him is inside the tollbooth, the other half hanging out the window. His feet are hooked into the steering wheel of his car, balancing him. He's young. Had a bit of a baby face. I felt sorry for making him look so serious, wrinkling up his soft skin, worrying over me. I didn't even catch his name—and here he is, hands in my pants, holding my legs open. I had this feeling like all of my insides were funneling through my crotch, emptying me out. I didn't even want to look down, see what there was of myself on the floor. I had my head held up toward the traffic, looking at my lane all full of cars. Seemed to stretch on for miles. The flow was all clogged, blocked by this one man's automobile.

By the time I heard Josey cry, I was beyond hurting. I was past pain at that point. Numb to it. Nothing could've knocked me down. This man—he'd cut the umbilical cord with his keys and now he's holding my child. He tells me he can drive me to the hospital, if I'd show him how to get there. I think I nodded. He places Josey in the toll basket, where people toss in their quarters, using it for a cradle while he helps me out of my booth, lifting me into his car. Once I'm inside, he picks Josey back up and hands her over to me. We're getting this poor man's upholstery all messy. I tried to apologize, but he wouldn't hear it. Before we drive off, he tosses in his fifty cents—getting the guard arm to let us through.

"Sorry for all this, sir," I said, the words sounding pretty distant. Small talk was all I wanted, I guess. Get my mind off of myself.

"Don't worry about it. What's your name?"

"Audrey. What's yours?"

"William," he said. "Got a name for the baby?"

Suddenly I remembered my favorite license plate. The name just rolled off my tongue, before I even thought over what I was saying. "Josey."

"That's a beautiful name for a girl."

He was right. Looking at her just then, I knew she was going to be the most beautiful girl in the world.

"She's going to make some guy a happy daddy."

"Not quite," I said, bringing her closer to my breast. "Unless you're interested." It was supposed to be a joke, but I guess it didn't sound like one so much. He got real quiet, tightening his grip on the steering wheel. Saw his wedding ring. It was crusted in my blood, the gold scabbed over with the rest of his hands. *Just my luck*, I thought. That's this job's biggest occupational hazard. No matter who I meet, everyone always leaves me behind. He dropped me off at the hospital, pulling up in front and helping me inside. I was whisked away before I could even ask him where he was heading, how I could repay him. This nurse took Josey out of my hands, while another wheeled me off into a room of my own. I got asked more questions than I can remember, having to answer everything from my name, my age, to who the father was.

"He just left," I said, figuring, it'd be best to believe this man had been her daddy. Fact of the matter is, whoever he was, this

William had done more for my child than anyone else. He'd make a better father for Josey than any of these other men passing through my tollbooth, which is just the way I want to remember him—driving up and taking me away, whisking me off from that dead-end job for good.

w i l l i a m   c o l b y

I always thought South Carolina was supposed to be a thin state. Figured I would've pushed through to the other side in no time. It's those tollbooths that kept me from getting anywhere. People are supposed to welcome you into their state, not charge you just to come in.

I've been collecting flies across the countryside. Whenever I have the window rolled down, it seems like I pick another one up. They're hitchhikers I never figured I'd take in—but they've been buzzing around my ear for the last ten hours now. Shelly's got a soft spot for pilgrimming insects. The first fly I found flitted in through the window just before the car crossed over the Carolina state line, landing on the dashboard by the speedometer. It scuttled over all the gauges, the fly's wings humming along with the engine—that slight vibration from its body going in perfect harmony with the car.

A couple miles later, I felt this itch at the nape of my neck.

Brought my hand up to swat at whatever it was, cupping a fly against my shoulder. I held it there for a second—feeling the fly twitter around, buzzing against my palm, crawling over my neck. I closed my fingers into my wrist, hoping to catch the fly in my hand. I pulled my hand away, feeling the hum of the fly inside. It could've been an engine in my hand, a motor fit for my fist, revving away. I reached my arm out through the window, lining it up parallel to the highway, and opened it—letting the fly go, the wind whisking it away.

Later, this hiss of wings zipped past my ear. My hand pulled up from the wheel and brushed the sensation off my neck, that jitter resonating through my skin.

Looking over to the passenger-side window, I saw a stretch of open field, all of it empty—save for these black clumps of dirt. Probably cow pies. There was so much of it, all amassed together. Once I noticed that the dung heaps seemed to be following me, rolling over the ground and raising up into the air—I did a quick blink, only to realize those piles of cow shit were really flies inside the car, scurrying over the window. I turned behind me, back to the coolers—only to find a sheet of scattered black dots wrapped around the plastic. They formed a blanket over the lid, continuously redefining their shape. The engine was having a hum-along with these flies. The dash was scattered with black bodies, the flies' wings looking like new, indecipherable numbers on all the gauges.

The sun's become unbearable. My air conditioner has been on the fritz ever since Virginia, turning this car into an oven. When I look at the highway, I can see the heat rising off the asphalt—the air actually bending under the temperature, warping into awkward shapes. We've gone through our spare already, popping the left rear tire somewhere around Florence, about fifty miles back. I had to step out and change it all by myself, nearly getting myself hit by the side of the road. Nobody driving by even slowed down for me, speeding past my back—the air picking me up and pushing me against the fender of my car. Once I sat back inside the car, I was sweating, covered in dirt. All I've wanted for the last fifty miles is a road motel—somewhere I can pull over and take a shower, pass out for a couple hours.

But we're on a schedule. We need to make it down to Florida by tomorrow or we'll miss our six-month anniversary. We've been married for half a year and we're finally getting around to having our honeymoon. Shelly wanted to celebrate at the southernmost corner of the country, which means I've got a little over twelve hours to reach Key West, or at least Kendell. That's close enough. Shelly will just make do with the Everglades. That park is big enough to get lost in. It takes up the entire tip of Florida. When you look at a map, it looks like a toenail painted green.

Shelly had her toes pedicured before, polishing them up in the same color. She dolled herself up the day before I shipped out, marking the occasion by giving herself a makeover.

"I waxed my bikini line and everything."

"How much does something like a pedicure cost?"

"You really want to know?"

"Sure."

"You're not going to like it."

"That much?"

"About forty dollars."

"Just for your feet?"

"Doesn't it look good, though? I mean, don't you think my feet look pretty?"

"Forty bucks isn't going to make your feet look any better than they already do."

She leaned over to me, opening her mouth over mine. Her lips sealed off my voice, her cheeks muffling up my intonation—

the words redirected down her throat, as if she were swallowing them. She started talking back to me, repeating whatever I said. Her voice rushed into my mouth, a hum running through my cheeks, a slight vibration in my lips. Whatever I had been saying got lost, the words reduced to their resonance. I pressed my face into hers, nearly tapping our teeth together—continuing to talk. It became less and less about saying anything specific—our jaws merely opening and closing in rhythm to one another, fanning back and forth. The air from her own lungs traveled into mine. Whatever we'd been arguing about was gone, gulped down and stomached.

Her chin was resting on my shoulder. Her words were weighed down with drowsiness, her voice drifting farther off. "Can you pick your favorite part of me?"

"My favorite part of your body?"

"When I'm not around and you close your eyes—what's the first piece of me that pops into your mind?"

"This sounds like a trick question."

"It's not, I promise. I'm just curious."

"It has to be something other than your breasts, right? I'm supposed to pick something like your eyes, aren't I?"

"You think about my breasts?"

"No, that's not what I'm saying. I *can't* think about your breasts first—even if they are my favorite. If I say I think of them before the rest of you, I'll be in trouble. That'll make me like every other guy who ogles their girlfriend's boobs. I'm supposed to separate myself from the rest. I'm supposed to say something more meaningful, more romantic. Right?"

"My breasts are your favorite part of me?"

"Shell, that's not what I'm saying—"

"Well, what is, then?" She pulled herself up onto her elbow, hovering above me. She gave a quick jiggle of her breasts, grinning as she shook. "Don't let me distract you or anything. Clear your mind of everything else . . ."

Her voice is passing through the air between us, the words dissipating into the atmosphere—solid with sound for that split second, then gone. I feel this tickle in my neck, her mouth so close to my skin that the sounds themselves leave an impression. It's as if she's stroking me with an invisible body part. Her voice, the essence of her breath. That's my favorite. Even if there isn't anything to see, even if it isn't tangible or physical—it's the part of her that I feel strongest about.

I thought of how I could hold on to her voice. I could take all the objects in our house that her intonation had entered. The mouthpiece to the telephone could have the residue of all her conversations crusted inside. If I twisted it off the receiver, maybe I'd find a film of phone calls still coating the inner rim. I could take her toothbrush, searching for those muffled bits of talk caught within the bristles. There were the coffee mugs that still had an imprint of her lower lip ringing the brim, that faint trace of Chap Stick or lipstick hanging down from the edge like a tapestry.

"You don't have a favorite part of me because I'm ugly. You just don't want to admit it to me . . ."

She's drifting away, not even aware of what she's saying anymore. We fall asleep while trying to sustain the conversation. We kept talking, the gaps between our thoughts widening—seconds into minutes, all the way into hours. I'd wake up in the dark, hours later, thinking we were still in the middle of our talk, and I'd get scared that Shelly would find out that I had been dozing off on her when I should've been listening. I'd try to wake myself up by nodding my head, mumbling, *yeah, uh-huh, yeah* . . . but there'd be no reply. Shelly was well off into her sleep. She'd been there for hours. I'd watch her mouth maneuver around her dreams, talking to someone in her sleep—only to slip away myself, dozing off again. Our bodies wound around each other, the two of us knotted in with our limbs—while I'd still hear her talking to me in my dreams, listing off which parts of her body were worth keeping, her breath wrapping her words within a warm receptacle of sound.

Tape recorders wouldn't work. They only captured her intonation. Hearing her voice was only half of it. There was the presence of her breath that packaged the sound, a sense of touch coming along with the words. A tape player could never catch that completely—like a butterfly net with a gaping hole at the end.

And what about the heat she'd leave on the sheets of our bed when she'd wake up in the middle of the night and walk to the bathroom? I'd run my hand across her side of the mattress, the warmth from her body resonating up from the blankets. How could I capture that? The impression would fade before she'd flush the toilet, the temperature dropping off from the cloth by the time she'd slip back into the sheets. She found my hand there, waiting for her to come back, placed right where she'd been sleeping. She almost lay on top of my arm before she realized I was palming her place in bed. She picked up my hand by my thumb, shaking it a bit, my entire arm flopping limply through the air.

"What's this?" she asked. "When did this get here?"

"I was looking for you."

"You found me."

"What time is it?"

"You don't want to know."

"That late?"

"Yeah. I keep waking up. Can't sleep so well."

"Again?"

"Yeah."

This time, I left her there. I was the one who fell back to sleep while she just sat awake for the rest of the night.

I'm afraid I'm beginning to forget these things. Moments are decomposing. Memories are molding over all the time now. You'd think a photograph would be enough to solidify a piece of your life, freeze-drying time forever, but I'll look at pictures of Shelly from years ago and won't be able to remember where they were taken. I can't even remember if I was the one behind the camera, snapping off the shot in the first place. It's as if I were looking at her through someone else's eyes—the lens too distant from the moment to make me feel like it was mine, that I had experienced this firsthand. The trouble with a camera is that it lets you collect the moment while setting you aside from experiencing it yourself. You might as well not have even been there, taking part in that second where the camera goes click, because it was more important to remember the moment later, to catalog it away in some scrapbook, when it could've just been better to have let the picture opportunity pass and live the experience for yourself, allowing your memory to do its job on its own, rather than prod it along with a photo.

I started thinking about all the remnants of Shelly shed throughout the house. Everything from clumps of her hair collecting in the bathtub drain, to snips of her fingernails in the trash can. They're the only things that I have left. I had to comb through the entire house, looking for the details of her under couch cushions, underneath the bedspread. All the way down to the dust covering the tabletops. In that residue, there were bits of her skin. If I rubbed my finger over the tabletop, half of the film covering my skin would've been fragments of her shed flesh—commingled with mine. Dust was the best place for us to be now, the only place where we were still together—our past blending into one entity, light enough to drift through the air and coat our entire house.

With enough of her hair clumped together, I could almost smell the shampoo she used—taking a handful and cupping it over my nose. The scent was so faint, I'd have to strain all of my senses just to pick up the slightest trace. But it was there, inside my palms. A faint wisp, inhaled and registered. If I had just enough fingernail clippings to match her hands, ten total, I could conjure up those moments when she'd scratch my back, scraping those places where I couldn't reach.

"Did I get it?"

"Higher."

"There?"

"Yeah, yeah—right there. Perfect. *Puur*fect."

"If this is all I needed to do to get you purring, then you're putty in my hands."

"Harder."

"I have you under my spell. You'll do anything I say now."

"Right there . . ."

"Your back's getting all scratched."

"I don't care. It feels so goooood . . ."

"God, it looks like you've been attacked by a cat."

The temperature hasn't been helping. I'm sweating all over, my clothes clinging to me. Night's been the only time when the heat won't eat away at the car. I've tried to drive as much as I can in the dark, staying awake by rolling down the window, turning on the radio. Sleep has been working its way into me for hours. My eyes have been getting heavier by the mile. The divider lines are all I have to follow—the backroads black, no street lamps overhead or other cars to light the way. I've had my high beams reaching out in front of me, scooping up each painted strip off the highway—netting them within the grille like a whale feeding on shrimp through murky ocean waters. It reminds me of nights out at sea when I could hear a whale song from miles away, a distorted call echoing just over the surface. There had always been something so lonely to the sound, I remember—a noise searching for a response. I could hear the yearning within it. I've been getting so drowsy at the wheel, there are moments when I think I hear that whale song just outside my window—the passing breeze slipping in through the crack of glass at my ear, giving pitch to the wind. I feel as if there are whales chasing me along the highway. We're all riding together, heading south for warmer waters. I'm being led by a trail of white plankton, their slender bodies lining up behind one another, one by one. The fender coerces those divider lines through the gritted teeth of the grille, swallowed and stomached without a need to even chew. *Follow the food*, I keep thinking. Let them take you wherever there is to go. I haven't eaten all day, this pit forming in my belly. My stomach turns over on itself, rummaging around for some hidden scrap to digest. I've needed to stop for hours now, needing to sleep. I can't focus on the road anymore. My head weighs more than it did before, always wanting to lean over toward the steering wheel. My chin hits my chest—and I snap my neck back up onto my shoulders.

"You nodded off on me, didn't you?"

"No, no—I'm up."

"You did, I saw you." Shelly slipped her hand onto my leg, twisting her wrist around the seat belt's slack until she had cinched my knees together. "What can I do to keep you awake?"

"Just talk to me for a while."

"Talk to you? Is that all? I can do better than that . . ."

We had been visiting her family, five hours away. Thanksgiving, I think. Five years in a row with her folks. The drive back home was always at night, which meant we'd make it back to our house by around three in the morning. Shelly would fight off her own drowsiness just to keep me company. I'd let her sleep most of the time, not wanting to wake her if she slipped off from me—listening to her slight snore. I'd look over to her, her body bundled up in the passenger seat, somehow sleeping with her head propped against the window. Her neck was stretched out to the point of snapping. The faint light from the dashboard gave her skin that green glow.

Everything outside the car was gone, the rest of the world disappearing into darkness, leaving her floating through a black backdrop. If a tire ever dipped into a pothole, her head would roll forward, the quick dip in her neck abruptly waking her up.

"Where are we?"

"We've got an hour to go. Go back to sleep."

"No, I want to stay with you . . ." She still sounded like she was asleep—the words heavy in her mouth, barely even budging beyond her lips.

"You were snoring, you know that?"

"I don't snore."

"We're almost there. I'll wake you up when we get home, I promise."

"You're going to leave me in the car."

"I won't, I swear."

"I don't trust you. I'll wake up in the morning, sitting right here—while you're inside, sleeping in our bed."

"Stay awake, then."

"You're going to get us in a car wreck. You've had your eyes shut for miles."

"I blinked."

"They were closed for seven seconds. I counted."

"Three, tops."

"The car was rolling off the road. You only woke up because the tires started kicking up gravel."

"You were dreaming."

"I don't dream about getting into car wrecks. That's morbid."

"Do you want to drive?"

"No. I want to keep you awake."

"Then who's going to keep you up?"

"You."

"How am I going to do that?"

"Think of something."

"I can't think of anything that would keep us from crashing."

"Fine. Give me the wheel." She reached out, lightly slapping my hand. "Give it to me. *Give it*." She kept smacking my knuckles with her palm, each hit getting harder until I let go. She leaned in toward me, her right hand gripping the steering wheel while her left slipped along the seat belt, coasting down the stretch of nylon at my chest. When she reached my waist, her fingers stiffened, her nails digging lightly into my pants.

"Keep your eye on the road," she said. There was nothing to see below the dim glow of the dashboard, everything beneath my chest left in darkness. It felt as if there was something small crawling around my crotch, Shelly's hand stumbling over the zipper of my pants, her fingers clawing at it.

"You awake yet?" she asked.

"Oh, up and at 'em."

"No, not quite," she said. "But give me a second."

My pants exhaled with one swift zip, the cool air from the open window drifting into the hollow. There was nowhere to look other than out the windshield, the car climbing up the divider lines, like rungs on a ladder, leading us deeper into the darkness.

"You want to take the wheel now?"

I did, unable to say anything.

"Dare you to step on it, Will."

I pinned the gas pedal between my heel and the car floor, the engine heaving forward. The divider lines blurred into one another. The space in between each painted streak now had a film of unfocused vision connecting them. The lines went by so fast, a gray area had formed inside each gap—a blurry ligament linking them all together. Every sensation in my body was mounting inside Shelly's hands, adhering me to this highway. The wind peeling at my ears, the smell of the engine burning fuel, the black sky surrounding us—all of my senses were taut and ready to receive the world around me, directing me forward. Things had never been this clear before, this exacting. I was feeling everything so purely, so precisely—a warmth suddenly spreading up from my waist and into the rest of my body—that I couldn't help but close my eyes, wanting to get lost in that moment.

When I opened my eyes again, Shelly was gone. The highway was bare. The crispness to the air had dulled itself down to decomposition again—the smell emanating up from the coolers, taking over the inside of the car.

Wait, I thought. *Go back a few,* as if this moment was part of some slide show. My memory was hooked up to some film projector where, if I blinked, maybe I could move back to the moment where Shelly was still there, intact, holding me, guiding me along the highway. I kept closing my eyes, squeezing them tightly together in hopes of dragging back that split second. Open—nothing but an empty highway. Shut—*please come back to me Shelly please come back to me*. Open—nothing but the divider lines. Shut—*please Shelly please come back don't go*. Open—nothing but the mile marker by the side of the road. Shut—*please Shelly don't leave me here again please please*. Open—

A deer hopped right into the high beams, stepping into the spotlight. It bowed to the cheer of my screeching tires. There wasn't enough time to swerve, the car embracing the animal. Its fur swelled up within the headlights, the color bleaching out from the intensity of the light—the brown drained into a pale white. Its eyes had found me through the windshield. Somehow, it was able to look over the headlights and see me on the other side of the glass. We had three seconds to stare at each other, (1) the black of its eyes swelling into yellow, (2) the yellow deepening into pink, (3) the pink darkening into red as the headlights rushed directly inside her irises.

When the deer hit the fender, I could see the hood ornament smack against her chest. Her neck extended upward upon impact. Her chin slapped the hood of the car. Her head seemed rooted to the hood, planting her chest in place. Now her tail end suddenly came into focus, folding up from behind her and rolling toward me. Her hind legs hooked into the air, hitting the windshield with enough force to shatter through the glass. When the deer reeled its torso in toward me, I had the sudden feeling that we were welcoming ourselves into each other's arms. The deer's legs were open to me, while my arms were still holding on to the steering wheel. She spun directly into the front seat, her back striking my chest with the force of two hundred pounds. I could feel my ribs squeezing out my breath, a storm of glass showering down.

On a cloudless night like this, there's always a chance of finding a shooting star. I had my eyes up, mouth open, jaw slack—extending the length of flesh in between my jawbone and shoulder. That strip of skin keeps so tender, a kiss there's like burying yourself into a pillow with a pulse. You can hold a heartbeat within your lips, the vibration pushing its way into your mouth. I started to imagine I could see constellations forming above me, the loose stars forming ligaments to one another—a white line like those painted on the highway reaching out from one star and connecting to the next. One cell now two cells, three now four, developing into a body directly over my head. Organs form, limbs branch out. A skeleton to keep every entrail in place. A body. A woman's. Shelly's.

She's kissing everything. Planting her lips hard against my skin, she tries to untangle herself from my seat belt. Her hands push against my chest. The pressure builds up over top of my ribs, my breath caught inside my lungs. My chest tightens, becoming unbearable—bringing me back to the car.

The deer's hind legs keep kicking me in the chest. We're struggling against each other, fumbling for control. I'm trying to steady the car, reaching out for the steering wheel on the other side of her writhing body. She bucks upward, hitting her head directly against the ceiling—only to tear open the upper interior. When she lands back in my lap, shreds of cloth come down with her. Butting her head against my seat now, she finally pushes past the gap between the front and back, squirming behind me.

The windshield's gaping wide open, the wind rushing into my face. I'm pulling in the reins, bringing the car to a complete stop. I get kicked from the back, the deer's feet punting up against my seat. She's still struggling for a way out of the car. There's enough glass scattered across her body to blend in with her eyes, the fragments as bright as her own irises. It's as if her body opened up a dozen different sockets, the gashes filled with shards of glass—eyeballs all over, all staring toward me. None of them are blinking. Her fur is tattered and bleeding.

Looking through the windshield, the first thing I see is a broken neon sign. The letters are dull, no light running through the bulbs—just the faint trace of The Henley Road Motel written over my head. There's a tap on my window. I turn to the left, only to see this kid—his knuckles knocking against the glass. He's staring right at me, expecting me to step out. An older man in a bathrobe is strutting toward us, tying the strap around his waist to hide his gut. "You okay, sir?"

"Think so. Just a little shaken up."

"Looks like you're not going anywhere tonight," the old man said, scanning my car. "Why don't we set you up with a room, worry about this tomorrow?"

A room. That meant a bed. A pillow. A mattress. Clean sheets. Clean *sheets*. A bath. A towel. The smell of soap. An ice machine. A soda machine. A glass with a paper dustcover on top of it. Turn it over and it becomes a coaster. Television. Free cable. Movies all night. A room for the night sounded just right. The honeymoon suite, please.

"You got a name, sir? For the guest book?"

"Colby," I said. "William Colby." Said it for the first time in a while. My name lumbered out of my mouth like a dying dog—just hit by a speeding car along the highway, crawling across the asphalt, reaching for the ditch by the side of the road, its tongue lagging out from its jaw. William Colby. Sounded like roadkill.

"We'll put you in room two tonight, William. Keep you close to the office, in case you need something during the night. How's that sound?"

Sounded so good, I wanted to cry. Just fall right over at their feet and thank God for saving me from the road for a while. Just get me out of that car, please. Just get me somewhere I can sleep.

I remember my room. I walked into a mustiness that'd been trapped behind clenched doors for Lord knows how long. The air felt septic. The floral print wallpaper was deteriorating around the edges. There was one window overlooking the parking lot, a yellow film forming at the corners of the glass. The carpet nearly crunched with each foot I set down, the woolen mesh brittle below my heels. A slightly cracked mirror stood propped up against the wall, leaning off of a dresser with one of its drawers flung open. Inside it, a yellowed bible. Dust had long since settled over its cover. When I nudged the book with a finger, scraping it across the drawer's belly, an imprint of where it was originally positioned shadowed the shift.

On top of the dresser, there was a television set. Turning it on, static rose up from the screen, the blue crinkle casting its color across my body. I looked up into the mirror to see myself submerged in a dull ocean of television—my skin and clothes saturated in the crackle and fuzz.

Didn't take long for me to think of the sea. No matter how long I'd been back on land, almost every moment tried to drag me off to the ocean again. I couldn't even look at myself in the mirror without seeing water all around me. The boy had scurried behind me to the bathroom, turning its light on. The fluorescent bulb struggled to warm up, the light slowly building up its electricity. He turned the faucet on to show that it worked, a steady jet of water slipping into the sink. Then he did the same with the shower. Turning the nozzle, a rattle of pipes resonated through the walls of the bathroom. After a dry heave of air from the shower's nozzle, a spit of brown water shot out. It hit the base of the tub and slid toward the drain. The off-color water faded from a rust into a clear stream, rinsing a bit of the grit coating the porcelain away.

"Is there anything I can get you?" he asked me.

The honeymoon suite. The word *honeymoon* had been rattling around my head for the whole trip, resounding even louder once we were inside the motel room. This was supposed to be me and Shelly's honeymoon.

The weight of days in the car was calling me toward the bed. I sat myself down on the edge of the mattress. Once my head hit the pillow, I knew I wasn't going to be able to stand back up. Sleep couldn't be but so far away. Found a remote control sitting on the bedside table. Tried using it without much luck, pressing every button before giving up. I flipped the remote over and found the corner where the batteries slip in. In opening it, I got the crust of acid on my fingers. Took a while for it to sting, but there it was—a burn that sunk into my fingertips, calling up memories of water mains and steam valves. I crawled over to the edge of the bed and switched the television on manually. Static crashed against the screen. First channel I came to was scrambled, the picture distorting across the screen. There was a woman, naked—her body lumped into the lower corner, only to warp upward, her head pulled toward the top, her neck stretching out beyond the spine. Her arms were swirling into pink and orange spirals over the right half of the television. Her legs disappeared, cut out by the camera angle—only to jump back into frame and then skirt away again. I saw an eye for just a second. A tuft of hair turned blonde then purple, back to blonde, then flashing green. This girl couldn't keep herself together, splitting apart and breaking down, only to form and lose shape all over again. Her neck would sever, her head floating over the top of the screen, while the rest of her body writhed below—a gap in between.

Turning the volume up on high, moans blossomed out from the television set, in tandem with the motion.

Probably had to pay the man at the front desk five bucks to unscramble the sex spread across the screen. Probably the only way this motel could keep itself in business was by charging traveling salesmen a pretty penny for porno films.

But watching it like this—nipped and cleaved, jumbled and disconnected—made sense to me. Suddenly there were more arms than one body could hold, gripping onto indiscriminate limbs. At one point it looked as if there were five people altogether, bodies blending into one another. I saw a split second of clear screen, this woman mounting a man, hips turning inward—only for the distortion to kick in once more, sweeping away what clarity had been there before, the screen ripping their limbs apart all over again. I couldn't tell whose body was whose, the arms and legs winding into one another. The panting had a rhythm. The moans would start on a low octave, only to rise up in intensity.

This was our honeymoon. Shelly and me finally had our first night in a motel together, far away from everything else.

I filled the bathtub up to the brim with cold water. There was some ice from the ice machine floating along the surface, striking against the porcelain with a faint *clink*. The nylon cooler had been holding its breath for most of the trip, the air only slightly seeping out from in between its teeth. Opening it up brought out the smell, the odor rushing out with a heavy exhale. The water rose with each limb I slipped into the tub, nearly spilling over the edge by the time I stepped in. The inflatable armbands kept her arm and legs floating along the top, bobbing up and down over the surface. My body was just as buoyant as she was. Surrounded by her, I slowly took the air into my lungs, held it, and eased my head underwater. I slid across the bottom of the tub, until my head went below. My legs stuck up from the surface, straddling the spigot. I kept myself in position by pinching my knees onto the faucet, the metal cold against my inner thighs. My throat tightened, my chest heavy with my breath. When my lungs couldn't hold on to the air any longer, I finally felt a finger tap at my shoulder. In the tub, her arm brushed up against the side of my head, her fingers nearly stroking my ear.

I stayed in the tub for the night, my skin pickling with the water. I just wanted to soak for days. The sea was about the only familiar body that felt safe to me now, the pressure against my flesh keeping me calm. I was beginning to wonder about what I'd done, afraid that we'd never make it to Florida. Shelly was in no shape to share the responsibility of driving, leaving me behind the wheel. Her limbs were dwindling, the rest of her body thinning down to a few parts. I could consolidate coolers now.

I wanted to apologize to her, to at least try and make her understand that I didn't know how else to take her with me. I'd spread Shelly over half of our honeymoon, inseminating the South with the seeds of her body. The only way I figured she'd keep with me would be to give her back to the ground, one bit at a time. What returns to earth sprouts out from it again. Since her limbs were so stiffened, I thought it'd be best to soak her in the tub overnight before I planted any more of her—soften her skin just enough to nurture her germination along.

I only told one man about my wife on this last trip overseas. Dr. Edward Carmichael, our medical officer—he had come up with this business venture to earn a little extra money on board the boat. He was probably one of the only men who even remembered that I was a member of the crew, that I even existed—my weekly checkups for scurvy ensuring me a bit of social contact. I would talk about Shelly and he would tell me about his days back on dry land, recollecting his old medical practice, before his license was taken away.

"This girl had come to me in secret," he said. "Asked if we could talk alone. She was hiding her belly beneath an oversized sweatshirt, which tipped me off right away. Twenty-three weeks pregnant. That's awfully close for an abortion. The father was a local boy. Both of them were no older than seventeen."

"Did you end up doing it?" I asked.

"Wouldn't you? She had nowhere else to go. It was past midnight by the time we started working—having to wait until her parents went to bed, the two of us sneaking into her family's boathouse. I could hear the waves washing underneath the dock. The tide was lapping at my knees where I knelt. The only light I could use was an oil lamp—the glow so dim, I had to squint to see two feet in front of me."

"What did you do with the baby?" I asked.

"Two days later, a fisherman reported that he'd found a fetus in one of his crab traps. He'd been pulling up his cages, only to find one of them bursting with blue shells. He always filled his traps with chicken necks, so imagine his surprise when he found this one baited with a baby—all those crabs clawing at its tender skin. No one else had the know-how to do something like this, so it wasn't hard to figure out who to point the finger at. Word got out over what I'd done, until most folks who I'd known for years wouldn't even talk to me anymore. Whatever families had asked me to deliver their children looked elsewhere for help, worried over what I'd do to their babies. My career had been crippled by a simple decision. But I'd saved this girl's life. She would've done it herself, I know it. Because of that, I was excommunicated from my own home. I was shunned by the people who I'd known ever since I was a child. I'd grown up in this town, for Christ's sake. I still had family there. Half of the children there were born by me, brought into this world by my very hands."

Working as first medical officer on board a ship was simple. All he needed to do to get the job was fib over a few questions, leave out a few truths on his application. The men who run these ships tend not to look too hard for faults. For the rates they pay, they'd be fortunate enough to find someone who even had a medical degree.

Carmichael had five years on board this boat under his belt by the time I met him, having traveled to parts of the world to which most people never even think of going. All of Europe, most of Asia. Even Africa. On shore leave, he and the boys would head to whatever watering hole would serve them the cheapest beer, which—it never failed—would always be the local brothel. Women would be sitting on the bar, legs crossed, waiting for the right sap to blow his earnings away all in one night. Women would walk over to their table, bringing them drinks and saying in their best broken English, *This one on the house*. It was the third or fourth that wasn't. But by that time, these boys could not have cared less over how much money they were spending. With a little girl in one hand and a watered-down saki in the other, these men were royalty. They would disappear for an hour, stepping upstairs to one of the private rooms lining the second floor—only to stumble back to the bar with an empty wallet and a headache.

Ed never partook in the pleasantries, knowing quite well what he would have to deal with back on the boat. Tomorrow morning, he'd have a line of guys knocking on his door—all of them scratching at their crotches. It would border on a near epidemic, half the ship seized by a rash. Depending on where they docked, Ed would be prepared for that country's most popular sexual contagion. Crabs were common in the Philippines, while herpes was Norway's best kept secret. Genital warts were rampant throughout lower Africa, while Ireland had its own special strain of good ol' gonorrhea.

What never ceased to surprise Ed was the range of ages for these working girls. He'd seen prostitutes who looked young enough to be the daughters of other prostitutes, mother and child working alongside each other.

"I've got a proposition for you, Will," Ed said to me one day, just after asking me to lift up my lip so he could see my gums. "Think you might be interested in earning some cash, no strings attached?"

I had to save up for the honeymoon. I had to buy those coolers.

"What would I have to do?"

"Almost eighty thousand women die every year of back-alley abortions, nearly thirty percent of the world denied the right over their own bodies."

That didn't stop many women from performing one on themselves, which led to internal bleeding, infection, death. Some would simply keep on working, hocking their wares throughout their pregnancy. He'd seen it firsthand through all the dives he and the crew would cozy up to for the night, finding a handful of young girls with their tummies bulging. Their going rate was cut in half, just to entice these drunkards into bumping against their bulbous belly. *The Preggars Special*, is what the crew called it. *Two for the price of one*.

It made Carmichael sick, hearing them talk like that. "Maritime law is the loophole that can make it safe for women to receive the help they need. Sail twelve miles out to sea and you're in neutral waters, where the only laws that matter are those of your boat's point of origin. Whatever country your ship's registered in, you abide by their decrees."

If it was illegal for women to even ask a doctor to perform an abortion, he said, then we'd go to them.

"What we can do is bring the girl back on board with us. We'll wait until we ship out that evening and perform the abortion while we're out of intercoastal waters. We drop her off at the next port we dock at. It's as simple as that. It'd be worth it to the girls. We'd be doing them a service, while earning a little more income on the side."

"Have you done this before?"

"Once. It worked fine. What didn't work was one of the crew walked in on me while I was cleaning up, asking me for some penicillin. When he saw the girl sitting on the checkup table, he thought I'd buggy-lugged some whore back on board. As contraband. For kicks." He leaned in closer to me, lowering his voice. "If I had someone to help me out—man the door and make sure no one's coming, helping me sneak the girl on board and make sure she gets off without anyone ever noticing—it could work. We could perform as many abortions on board as we want. Depending on how many women we find needing help, we could bring them back one at a time or all at once. No one's really looking for something like this, so it'd be simple enough to just slip them on deck. Walk straight back to my office and have at it. We could earn a couple hundred dollars a night. I need a nurse with sea legs, Will—someone who can lean in with the waves while they work, bending their knees to keep balance."

The first girl we brought on board couldn't have been any older than sixteen. We had docked somewhere in South Asia, I forget which country—all the crew rushing to the nearest bar the moment the ropes were all tied.

She had plump cheeks. That's what I remember about her. Dumpling cheeks. The language barrier hadn't been as much of a problem as I thought it would've been. For every country we came to, Carmichael had practically picked up the language—collecting enough foreign tongues to speak to just about anyone we offered our services to. This chubby girl waddled over to us, sweet-talking me with what little English she had.

"Good time, boys? Good time?"

I only lowered my head into my beer as Ed leaned over, whispering into the girl's ear. Her face went from anxiously seductive to absolutely mortified. Standing back, she braced her belly—shielding her stomach with her hands. Ed said more, a little louder this time—enunciating something that I couldn't understand. I had no idea what he could've said to her to make her understand our little hackneyed operation. Standing in this bar, surrounded by more little girls than an elementary school playground, all of them swaddled in neon light, laughing and tossing their hair, straddling men twice their age, men who could've been their fathers from previous trips—I felt like I was going to retch.

When the girl agreed, Carmichael told her to wait with me while he sifted through the rest of the bar to find a few more. As we waited, I would try not to look at her—not wanting her to feel ashamed or embarrassed or whatever she might be feeling just then. We'd make eye contact for a brief second—and I'd see how much younger she looked when she wasn't trying to be seductive. She looked thirteen to me now.

We brought three girls back on board with us. There was very little if any talk between the five of us. It made me feel like I shouldn't be here. But I was the watchman. I had my job to do—stand outside Carmichael's office and make sure no one came in—while he took the three women inside, locking the door behind him. If any of the crew needed medical help—either a cure-all for a hangover or an ointment to counteract an itch, I had to tell them to come back tomorrow. I had to come up with some story about how there had been an accident on board, that Carmichael was in the middle of an emergency operation right now—either dressing a puncture wound or salving a second-degree burn or popping someone's eyeball back in the socket. Anything to get the crewman to walk away.

This is what Ed had told me before our first excursion into the world of intercoastal abortion. It hadn't occurred to me why Carmichael really needed my help. At first, I figured I was just a lookout. What he really needed was a place on board the boat that was less conspicuous than his office. He needed my boiler room.

Since my work was done alone, all at night, Ed saw me as the one person on board who could give him access to a private operating room, performing his abortions well belowdeck, far away from anybody hearing or seeing anything. I looked back to all those times when I had mouthed off to him about how lonely it was down there, how no one ever set foot down there, how I was completely and utterly on my own down there—while all along, this plan was forming in Ed's head.

He now had his private practice back. He was an intercontinental doctor.

Carmichael had customized our cargo freighter, converting the lower deck into his own nautical operation room—complete with examining table, jerry-rigged gynecological stirrups, a suction and curettage device.

And a storage facility. Nothing but a rubber bin left empty, ready for our little stowaways.

I noticed how the girls looked once the abortion was over. They seemed to be older. I'd seen these women run the gamut of ages, all in one night. They started off acting older than their bodies allowed them, eventually shedding the seductive demeanor for a more childish pose—only to end up with more years weighted upon their faces than they could've lived through, their eyes dragged down with gray bags, their lips drooping.

The first girl to go downstairs—the first girl to come up to Carmichael and me—her cheeks looked deflated now, her youth fizzling out. She kept her hands on her stomach, still shielding her womb from me.

Carmichael didn't finish until three in the morning. Once he was done, I had to head downstairs and return to my real work. The gauges still needed to be checked, the water pressure needed to be leveled. I wouldn't reach my bed until six or seven in the morning.

The air had changed belowdeck. There was a new smell hanging in the atmosphere—a scent similar to my own burning skin, yet stronger. More acrid. It smelled like flesh, spiced with something more fecund. More placental. The odor lingered around me for the rest of the trip. Whenever the water main let off steam, this high-pitched spurt of wet air spitting into the open, it sounded like a baby crying. I'd be walking through the hull, surrounded by miles worth of pipes, and suddenly I'd hear some child wailing away, squealing at my ear. I'd turn around and find nothing there. Just enough tubing to feel like I was caught somewhere along the birth canal, tangled inside the womb of some enormous mother. I thought I'd never get out. I thought I was going to be locked inside the bowels of that boat forever.

We were a family haunting this boat, the sound of these children resonating through the metal, echoing through the ship.

I funded this honeymoon with a hundred abortions. There was a tempest of feathers over my head when we set sail, a swarm of seagulls following us out to sea, as if the smell of placenta was in my skin, seasoned with the salt from the ocean air. That flock of white vultures hovered above our boat from the moment we performed our first abortion.

Your ears get used to that constant squawking. Mine did. It was the closest thing we had to someone cheering us on, as if those seagulls were supporting Dr. Carmichael's cause—clucking above the crew every day, seeming to say, *You're doing the right thing, guys. We're just here to offer you up a little encouragement.* But those birds were only after our cargo. We both knew that. At sea, I'd watch fishermen cast out their coat hangers almost every day—scraping at the water's womb. I've seen this ocean hollow out, right before my very eyes. The Atlantic had become so barren for me, staring at nothing but waves all day. The ocean was so infinite, we could've spent years sailing the seven seas and never come back. Our arrival would be marked by the cries of petrels, sending a warning to the people to bring their pregnant out to port. Those rubber bins would begin to fill themselves. We'd be risking mutiny, that heap of fetuses eventually outnumbering our own crew.

the henley road motel: ted henley

The vacancy sign up front hasn't worked for years now, ever since I was a kid. The burned-out neon looks more like bones brought up from a fire. Even when there was only a little marrow of light left in them, you could still see the name of this place flickering as far as five miles down the highway.

The Henley Road Motel. That was us. My father's name and my grandfather's name—mine, too—was just about the only thing you could see driving along Route 52. The red lettering hung in the air, luring in more moths than customers. If you ever stood near it at night, you could hear the hum of electricity flowing through, the current circulating from one word to the next. In a pulse, almost. Since it shorted, that sign simply stands next to the highway—a tombstone to my family's pride. Droops down to the asphalt a little lower every year.

One night runs you ten dollars. That includes towels. Checkout's at eleven tomorrow morning. Pets are welcome, if you own one. Just don't forget them when you go.

Posey was this stray some lodger had left behind in room four. Found her while changing bedspreads after checkout one day. She was the only pet I ever had with a heartbeat. Never needed to keep track of that damn cat. She always stuck around. Spent her time lazing underneath the sign, curling up inside its shadow. She'd only move to follow the shade, shifting with the eclipse throughout the afternoon. Never stood up for anything else.

The burned bugs littering the parking lot made that sign something of a buffet for birds, I guess. Rust had been rankling over its post for years, eventually opening up a sore at the lower left corner. A family of robins had slipped in, building their nest inside. Its hollowness reverberated their chirps, as if there were a hundred hatchlings infecting our family name—a feathered epidemic spreading underneath the fiberglass.

Posey's ears pricked up every time she heard wings above her head, following the faint trace against the back of the No Vacancy light. Wasn't until sunset one day, when my father flicked the switch, a rush of electricity flooding our name—that Posey's throat opened up into this caterwaul sounding *sooo* human, you'd think she'd been begging for mercy. Somehow, she'd climbed up that post, wriggling her way through the hole. Must've wrapped up into the wiring, tangling herself in tight. I had run out just in time to see sparks start sprinkling against the inner wall, these flashes of light flaring up underneath the fiberglass. Heard those birds, too, sealed inside—underlining Posey's cries with a layer of their own nervous chirping. A shrill peep from every beak, boiling over into a high-pitched crackle. Like fire. The lettering had begun to flutter, the intensity of the light wavering—while a new glow inside the sign started to grow brighter. It was a more natural light, not neon. But flames. A flush of orange in the far corner, mounting in size. My damn pussycat was on fire.

The blaze had rushed over every bird, a sudden hush running through. Couldn't hear them anymore. I pictured those robins wilting over each other, like flowers exposed to too much sun. Tongues lit like wicks, I imagined their beaks filled up with a mouthful of fire.

I remember seeing the last bit of light lingering in our name, the neon drained of its life—until the only light that was left was Posey's own burning body. Smoke spilled out from the opening, the smell of barbecue spreading through the whole parking lot. Once there wasn't any skin left to kindle the flames, Posey just drifted off into cinders—her glimmer sinking into ash.

Dad didn't see much reason in fixing the sign. Our customers had dwindled down to post-prom parties at that point, so he just left it the way it was. He wouldn't even let me pull Posey out. Her bones are still in there, I bet, some five years later. Probably all piled up in the corner, as dappled as a worn-out lightbulb.

Not that I didn't get my fill of dead animals. Look at that highway. Pretty much all that ever sticks around this place is what gets run over. Everything else drives away.

I got used to making company with what I peeled off the pavement, though. Had to. It was my job. My father would pay me a quarter for every possum I pulled up from in front of the motel, hoping to keep the parking lot clean for customers. Wherever they were. It'd be easy enough to earn five bucks each week. As long as I could keep myself away from the vending machines, I could've saved up fifty dollars by the end of summer.

That's what you inherit if you're a Henley—business sense. The means in which to milk a market out of nothing. And I mean *nothing*. All it ever takes to find your vocation is a vision. And I saw a new opportunity sprawled across the pavement every day. If pickings were slim, I'd sneak farther down the highway with my pail and spade. Wouldn't come home until I'd filled that bucket up to the brim with roadkill. They pop up in crops along the asphalt, these lumps of fur flourishing out from the highway. Could've been flowers growing out of the road. Each had a stem of bone, their spines holding a head of red petals—brains blooming out from their split skulls. Finding a patch was as easy as following the smell, the aroma of decay floating through the humid air.

I'd bring home a bouquet for my father almost every day. If it was flat, he could've cared less where I'd picked them up. He was happy enough to see me keeping busy, I guess. Working on something. He'd tally up how many critters I had, sifting through his pockets for some spare change.

I was making more money than the motel was.

A couple more summers like those and I would've earned enough to buy my own automobile. Didn't matter what brand, what model. Could've cared less about the color. If it had an engine, then that car would've been good enough for me. I stuffed my piggy bank up to its gullet with quarters, fattening it on my savings until it choked. Had to move on to mayonnaise jars by the time I was fifteen. I couldn't make enough ham sandwiches to keep up with my own earnings, spreading my bread with a thick layer of Hellmann's at every meal—until I sickened myself on that suet.

A bus ticket would've been simpler, sure. I'd saved up enough money to get Greyhound to take me just about anywhere. But once I reached wherever I'd gotten, where would I go from there? Know what I mean? I'd just end up stuck in some other town, worse off than I was here.

But a car is a skeleton key to this country. It unlocks every road, opens up every state. There isn't anywhere I wouldn't have been able to go if I had my own automobile. Didn't have a plan or someplace in mind where I could've gone. Running away was all I knew I needed to do.

I'd been born into this motel. My name was on that sign, which meant this would all be mine by the time my father retired. I would've inherited ten vacant rooms, rusty plumbing. Dusty bedspreads. I could change sheets that never got used anyhow—keeping up the routine just to save myself from going crazy. Could've spent my days watching the color in the curtains fade from too much sun, the dye drained down to its last drop—like blood leaking out from some run over raccoon.

Or I could leave it all. Just up and drive off one day.

When you look down either end of this highway, all you're liable to find is more asphalt. See? The pavement runs right on into the sky, as if the road could lead you there in your automobile. You could drive directly into the sun as it set, I bet, if you timed your trip right. Park on top of some sunspot and make your way around the world. And I'm sure you'd find yourself someplace—*anyplace*—a hell of a lot happier than here.

So I started planting roadkill. My field was ten feet of highway. God's acre was mine now, two empty lanes of pavement parched for the harvest. I'd sprinkle a thin layer of garbage across the divider lines, fertilizing the asphalt just before going to bed. Staying awake at night, I'd strain my ears to hear the hum of an engine. The gentle rush of rubber rolling over the road always sounded like rain to me, so I'd hold my breath at the faintest spread of tire treads. Just praying for it to storm. As it passed, if I heard a break within the coasting of the car—just a simple lapse in that rubber monotony, where the wheel lifts up from the pavement, the two parted by the body of some trapped animal, a *thump* punctuating the impact—then I knew I'd wake up the next day to a quarter's worth of carcass.

Harvest season was every morning for me. And I cultivated crops of all kinds. Raccoons, possums, squirrels. Even snakes. I reaped these trees for every animal they had, turning a profit from my own father's pocket. He couldn't keep up with me. Had to knock my wages down to a dime for every head, after a while. Then a nickel. Supply had oversaturated demand, the market just as drenched as the highway was with blood.

To keep my business afloat, I needed to start supporting my father's.

Then it hit me. Best damn business plan I ever had.

These woods were ripe with deer. Every morning, I'd wake up before the sun, just to pry off last night's meal ticket. I'd sift through mist as thick as a muffler's exhaust, the wet grass sticking to the soles of my pajamas. But when daylight'd break, I'd see that these weren't just trees, but there were antlers blending in with the branches. I'd find a family of deer scattered around me, the dark bleeding out from where their horns hooked through the sky draining the night into a pale morning. If I took my steps gently, none of them ever seemed to mind me. Wasn't until a car would pass that the deer would disappear deeper into the woods, leaping through the tangle of trees with the ease of swimming about a body of water.

It got me thinking. The number of drunkards rubbing their Firestones down to stubs on this highway was so huge, littering the ditches with their half-empty beer cans. You could smell the reek of rotten fur and rusty alcohol for miles. When a deer ducks under your car, there's enough damage done to strand you at the side of the road for good. An antler could rip into the hood of your Hyundai like a can opener chewing through aluminum. Slam into a buck and your fender is going to fold right around its fur like arms opening up for a hug. Consider yourself walking after that, trust me.

But what better place to have an accident than in front of the Henley Road Motel? What could accommodate you better than a roadside oasis like this?

If it hasn't rained for months, to save his crop, a farmer's gonna irrigate, right?

Well, one night, as soon as my father had fallen asleep in the office, I tiptoed out into the woods. Crouched down about a few yards back from the highway. Sat there for an hour or so, until the deer started seeping out from the trees, just like snails oozing out of their shells. A fawn finally made her way up in front of me, stepping in between me and the road. I didn't move. Hardly even breathed. Simply squatted there, watching her. She had eyes the size of dimes. The moon had polished her fur with such a sheen. She looked silver to me, colored in her own chrome. I began to imagine the twists her body would take upon impact, conjuring up contortions she'd wind up in. That's the Henley business sense for you, right there. *Envision your success and success will follow.* That fawn's body became a furry whirligig in my mind—her hind legs heading in one direction, her upper torso in the other. Until her limbs had no angle they couldn't make.

An automobile is a release from Mother Nature's restraints. Nature could take the body but so far, before one's own bones blocked the way. But a car could unlock the elbow, jog those joints free—bending the body beyond its limitations. It was the only unnatural ingredient in growing my bone orchard. A fertilizer of fenders. Add a dash of that to the asphalt and the roadkill would crop up constantly. *That* was my vision. *That* was my *dream*.

When a car finally came down the highway, I waited in place. Held out for the moment when its high beams lit up within the deer's eye, a pink shine filling in that black. I stood up just as the headlights were about to pass, scaring the fawn forward. She lunged out from the trees, a single leap over the ditch and into the road. Tires started to skid, melted rubber buttering up the highway. And *smack*—I saw that fawn tuck her head under the car's fender. Flipped her hind legs into the air in a somersault, laying her back flat across the hood. The metal rippled below her body, like a puddle of water that wouldn't break, refusing to let her go below the surface. Bouncing off the hood, she spun toward the windshield.

And *crash*. The crackle of glass might as well have been the cash register ringing up another customer.

My father ran out of the office wearing his ratty bathrobe, only to find me helping this driver from his crumbled car. "You all right there, sir?"

Couldn't have been a more confusing question for the man. He nodded his head, unaware of what he was even answering. His face was scraped up pretty good. Couldn't make out his features from underneath all those cuts, wearing a mask of his own blood.

"Looks like you're not going anywhere tonight. Why don't we set you up with a room, worry about this tomorrow?"

Another nod from the man, just as bewildered as before.

"You got a name, sir? For the guest book?"

"Colby," he says. "William Colby."

"We'll put you in room two tonight, William. Keep you close to the office, in case you need something during the night. How's that sound?"

He nodded again, same dip in the chin like all the others. We could've asked him just about anything, and he would've agreed.

After the man paid his deposit, my father put down a dollar

on the counter for me. I'm not lying. The whole bill, all mine. Never made more than a quarter off of any chore before. Nearly lost my jaw, it dropped so fast. But when I reached for my pay, Dad dropped his hand over mine, pinning my palm to the dollar. His face suddenly flushed with as much blood as his cheeks were gonna hold. Thought he'd pop if he didn't say something soon. He simply stared me down, his eyes brighter than a pair of high beams, until I was blinded by what was on his mind, whether he said anything to me or not.

He knew what I'd done. I could see that. It was simmering beneath his cheeks—this burning realization that I was a better businessman than him.

"Bring the car 'round back," he muttered, letting me go. "Bad for business, leaving that wreck up front."

I didn't argue with him. Simply ran right out of the office with that soggy dollar stuck to my palm, soaked in my own sweat.

I remember the highway sparkling under the moonlight. Shattered glass had scattered across the run of the road. Looked as if I was staring into a pond, the dark water reflecting the stars overhead. Felt like I was in between two spaces, neither here nor there. Not anywhere. Our motel was sitting smack-dab in the middle of some black hole, leaving me in a limbo.

The windshield had burst open in front of the steering wheel, sending a web of cracks throughout the rest of the glass. That fawn had thrust herself through the window, actually slipping into the car. Found her in the backseat, her body all knotted. Her head was tucked between her haunches, her two front legs bow-tied to her neck. Kept looking at her through the window, watching her twitch. She was covered in glass, every quiver catching the moonlight in these silver ripples.

I felt compelled to touch her. To feel her pulse and remember what it was like to handle an animal that's still alive. I opened the rear door and sat down next to her. Started stroking her side. My palm went wet with her blood, still warm.

Know what that feels like? I'll tell you. Go through the parking lot and find the one automobile that's leaking oil. If the car just pulled in, that puddle's gonna have some heat to it. The temperature implies *life*. You have the chance to hold existence in your hand just before it fades, going cold forever. And here I was, cupping this vital spark, feeling it drift away the longer I held on to it. I didn't want to let it go. With a car, you can always pour in more of whatever it's bleeding. Fix your automobile right up. So why would a body be any different?

I slid my hand up the run of her neck. Cut myself on a shard of glass hiding in her fur, bleeding right back at her. *Into* her, like an oil change. After petting her for a while, I swear, that fawn finally kick-started back to life. She went into this fast spasm in my lap, jumping right up to her feet. Looking straight at me, her eyes were as wide as silver dollars. I had a second's worth of time to stare down two bucks before she dove over me, leaping through the open door. Just flew out into the highway, collapsing when she landed. Her legs wouldn't hold her anymore—they were so broken. But she picked herself up from the road and ran, only to drop over again. Wobbled her way into the woods, eventually, the trees swallowing her whole.

I didn't chase after her. Didn't feel the need, really. I'd gotten my dollar, so. Kept to the car, instead.

I'll be honest with you, here—that was my first time in an automobile. Never had the chance to sit inside one before, especially not alone. My father's broke down years before I ever had the itch to slip behind the wheel. So I crawled into the front seat of this one, latching my hands around that power steering. I simply slipped my body into place, attaching each limb like a ligament to its proper pedal. The upholstery shifted into sinew, the seat molding over me. Hey—I was the skeleton to this new skin. Wore that car like flesh fitting over the bone. And it fit perfectly. Found the keys in the ignition, just tempting me to twist. I couldn't resist. I switched that automobile on, sending a shudder up from the engine, passing directly through the upholstery into me. The vibration eased this ache out of my spine, massaging my muscles. Felt heavenly, I swear. Reminded me of my father cradling me as a baby, lulling me to sleep by humming some song. The lullaby would vibrate through his body into mine. And I would just drift off into dreams, sailing away on my father's rolling throat. The tremble of the engine against my skin felt like his body pressed to mine, holding me all over again.

I could've just driven that jalopy off right then. Let that car take me anywhere it wanted to go.

Then I found my name hanging above the highway. Saw the front sign through the hole in the windshield, dangling over my head. The beacon of our family business stood like some soot-soaked scarecrow slung over an empty field, left with nothing to protect but pavement.

The Henley Road Motel.

That was me.

Heard the muffler scrape pavement as I pulled the car into the parking lot, the exhaust pipe raking through the gravel.

Couldn't fall asleep all too well that night. Counting sheep didn't help. I simply scraped them off my skull, one by one. I plucked them up from the highway in my head, until I was standing next to a mound of mangled animals, towering over me. Year's worth of roadkill had culminated into this: a throne of broken bones, adorned in organs, furbished with fur, trimmed in entrails. I was king to this highway, ruling over a court of roadkill. Grabbing onto a different rib, I climbed all the way up the pile, perching myself on top. Looking out along the horizon, I could see the rest of this country, *my land*, only to find every highway and interstate branching out from right where I sat. All roads led back to this motel. Wasn't anywhere I could've gone that wouldn't bring me back here. I'd never leave.

So I jumped. Leaped off my divan of dead animals with my arms outspread. I fell so fast, the motel began to expand below, growing larger the farther down I dove. Every room opened its door—ten mouths famished for me, like I was a worm dangling over a nest of hungry hatchlings. I woke up just as my body exploded across the parking lot, each room pecking at a different piece of me, swallowing their own limb.

Now I knew how my father must've felt when his dad stranded him with this business.

I found him in the office that morning, wearing his bathrobe for the fifth day straight.

"Third Saturday in May, son," he said. "Know what that means."

I did. It meant we were going to have our hands full with prom that night. For twenty dollars a key, we'd turn a blind eye to ten rooms' worth of drunk high-school students. Since we were fifteen miles out of town, we were the safest place for kids to smuggle in their alcohol. None of them minded paying twice the normal price. What did those kids care? They had their parents' money to burn. We knew it was worth every dollar to them, too—'cause they *sure* were positive we wouldn't call the sheriff on them if things ever got out of hand. Couldn't, really. Not with what they were paying. We wouldn't even dare.

Only duty I had that day was to freshen up the rooms. Took the entire afternoon to clean each one. Dusting curtains, washing windows. Room two was still occupied. I knocked on the door to see if Mr. Colby needed some clean sheets. Called out, *Room service, sir*—but nobody answered back. Peeking through the window, I could see that the bed had been used. Blankets were tossed off to the floor. Looked empty, otherwise. I figured Mr. Colby must've been an early riser, deciding to take a walk somewhere. Since he hadn't checked out that morning, my father put him down for another night—not even thinking twice about the man. We were about to partake in the busiest evening out of our entire year.

Our night got under way with the crackle of gravel, the parking lot crumbling under a hundred tires. I'd never seen so many cars. Not at our motel. Once the doors started opening, a hail of empty beer cans tumbled to the ground—the hollow ring of aluminum chiming through. Up popped every trunk, another kid pulling out a different kind of cooler. I could hear the clink of bottles inside, swirling in a puddle of melted ice. You could tell those high-schoolers were drunk already, stumbling around. The boys looked all dapper in their tuxedos, their undone bow ties dangling from their collars. Made them all look like their throats had been torn out, the skin still clinging to their necks. Most girls were wearing these strapless evening gowns, showing off their shoulders. They had their corsages wrapped to their wrists, as if their veins had sprouted flowers, blossoming out from their hands.

I tried picturing them differently. But they all looked run over to me.

We'd never been this busy before. Ever. Thought it'd make my father excited, doing this much business. But he never looked up from the register. Just rang up each room, handing over every key. Once we were full, he went ahead and flicked the switch to the front sign. Which struck me as kind of funny. Nothing happened, of course—save for this slight crackle of electricity. A couple sparks spit out from the burned neon and that was about it, as if the sign was insulted from my father letting these kids stay in the first place. I don't even know why he did it. Never had the chance to ignite the No Vacancy light when it was working, so I figured maybe he just wanted to reap what pride he could feel from finally filling this place up to the hilt for once.

"We're running a dead motel, son," he said, flipping on his television set. "These rooms just don't know it yet. We'll be out of business by next month."

He turned the volume up high, drowning out the racket. I didn't see much point in sitting with him in the office. Decided to take a walk, instead. See what I could find. Passing each window, I heard everything from bottles breaking to girls squealing. Every room harbored its own debauchery. If this was a dead motel, well, then death seemed pretty lively to me. More alive than I ever felt.

When I reached room nine, the curtains had been left open just enough to peek in. Saw this girl passed out in the bed, her silver dress hiked up to her waist. She wasn't wearing any panties. Still had her corsage on, though. The strap, at least. The petals had all fallen off, sprinkled around her. She wasn't moving much, just lying there. There was this boy in the far corner of the room, hovering over a table filled with empty bottles. He fished up a can of beer and swallowed what liquor was still in it, crushing the metal in his hands before tossing it to the floor. The clatter woke her up. She reached right for her head, wincing when she touched her temples. Then she said something to the ceiling. Asked it a question, I think. I couldn't hear her. The boy turned his head just enough to yell at her. Told her to shut up, loud enough for me to hear from the other side of the window. That got her crying. Lifted her knees up to her stomach, wrapping her arms around her legs.

Something about her posture felt familiar to me. Couldn't place it at first. I knew I'd seen a bundle of limbs like that before, somewhere. Wasn't until she *really* started sobbing, sending herself into these slight convulsions, that it struck. She reminded me of my fawn from last night. She had balled up her body just like that deer, her silver dress a perfect match for its fur. I got so excited, the window fogged up in front of my face. Couldn't see inside anymore. My own breath was blocking the way.

But before I could wipe off my exhales, I felt this tap at my shoulder. Turned around to find this footballer standing behind me, having a hard time keeping his balance. He had a bottle in his hand, half of its alcohol soaked into his suit. "You work here, don't you?"

His breath reeked of roadkill. Every exhale left him smelling like he'd been run over for months. Had to nod my head at him, just to duck away from the flow of air.

"I was wanting to take a shower, but there's no soap, see? I thought this place came with some soap, some free shampoo." He took a step forward, jabbing his beer at me. Saw some grit swirling in his last swallow, a piece of gravel from the parking lot rolling around the bottom of his bottle. "Can I get my complimentary shampoo, sir? *Please?*"

Just as my mouth opened to answer, this yell forced its way out into the air. Not from my mouth. Someone else's. A girl's throat. I turned in time to see my fawn pointing at me through the window, shielding her body with the bed's blanket. I made eye contact with her boyfriend just before he ran outside. Gripping this empty beer bottle by its neck, he smashed it against the door, leaving a jagged green ring jutting up from his fist. He held out a bouquet of broken glass for me, thrusting it right into my face.

"What are you peeping at, pervert?"

Now how could I answer that? I kept my attention on that

bottle, each shard catching a different porch light—the glass shining in a green glow. The first rule of running this motel was to leave the customers alone. I'd promised my father to keep clear of these kids, let them do what they wanted. But that drunk footballer gripped both of my arms from behind, throwing me to the ground. The two of them started punting me across the parking lot, kicking me in the stomach. The air wouldn't stay inside my lungs long enough to draw out the oxygen. Their shoes kept knocking at my chest, forcing every breath out from my mouth. I was getting fuzzy in the skull, my focus drifting from my eyes. Heard the doors to every room open, a horde of tipsy kids pouring into the parking lot. A crowd had formed, I could see them. A group of girls were all gawking at me, *but where were the boys?*

Felt another foot dig into me just then, at my back. Someone was stomping on my leg. Got a kick in the throat. Looking up, I saw enough cummerbunds to form a perfect circle, a mobile of undone bow ties dancing over my head. Just like I was a little baby, lying in my crib. Must've had the whole football team on top of me, each kick stinging like a cigarette butt put out on my skin.

Heard a bone snap. Couldn't tell where, but the sound of it had my whole body to echo through. Got the heel of someone's shoe in my mouth, my front two teeth folding backward—my tongue welcoming the rubber sole inside.

So this was what it felt like to get run over, I'd say. My body embraced the notion—finally getting a feel for what I'd based my family fortune on. I deserved this, I guess.

Felt good to get wet, the rush of beer and whiskey showering down on me. That boyfriend from room nine told everyone to stand back. He lit a match as the alcohol kept coming, raining from all over—until the liquor began to burn. Set fire to every scrape I had. Reminded me of Posey, her flesh feeding the flames from the front sign, wrapped in a sheet of heat. I rolled and rolled and rolled, trying hard to snuff out the fire feeding through my clothes. I could just barely see the burned neon looming over those boys' heads, watching as all this happened. Watching me get mine. Made me think of my grandfather building this motel fifty years ago, before I-95 leached the traffic right off Route 52. He worked here to the day he died, you know that? Never left this place once.

I seriously doubt it would've ever let him go.

Thank God those kids finally got bored with me. Once they'd dredged up every bruise my skin was going to give, my clothes all charred, they dropped their empty bottles and ambled back to their rooms. Each boy grabbed hold of a different girl, dragging them off. I was probably crying, but I couldn't tell. I was numb from soaking up so much alcohol. The corners of my lips felt crispy, all parched. I couldn't even feel my own mouth anymore.

Took awhile to peel myself off the ground, but I dragged my body back to the office. Found my father still at his desk, watching his TV like nothing had happened.

Look at what they did to me, Daddy, I said, just barely hearing myself over the laugh track of some sitcom. I was so lightheaded, I thought they all were laughing at me.

They hurt me. They tried to burn me.

"Go wash yourself off and head to bed."

But look at me, Daddy. You got to do something.

"Shouldn't have been messing with the clientele. You know better than that."

But I didn't do anything to them—

"What did I tell you?" He finally turned to me, staring right into my eyes. Wouldn't look at the rest of me, locking his sight on the only part of my body that wasn't bleeding. "The customer has always got to be right. You're gonna have to learn that. Now clean yourself up and go to sleep. That's the end of it. I don't want to hear another word about it."

My face suddenly flushed with as much blood as my cheeks were gonna hold. Felt my scabs crack back like mouths opening up to vomit, spitting out fresh blood. My father had charged twenty dollars for nine rooms, ten for room two. He had made one hundred and ninety dollars that night. More money than we'd earned all year. Forget his pride. He'd burned that up a long time ago.

All I wanted was to hide. Go someplace where I knew no one would find me. I helped myself into room two by using my father's skeleton key. Only place I figured I could go.

I walked into a mustiness that smelled as if someone had been living in there for years, never cracking a window once. Every breath that'd been exhaled inside was still lingering around, the flavor of old oxygen filtered through a dozen different mouths. Place was vacant, otherwise. I took a shower, rinsing away all the dirt and blood. My body was a bouquet of bruises—purple, red, black and blue. Tried sniffing each injury to figure out what kind of flower I smelled like. The bridge of my nose had broken, so I couldn't tell. Hurt too much to slip my clothes back on, so I wrapped a towel around my waist and hobbled over to the bed.

People try to leave behind the pieces of themselves that they're most ashamed of, seems to me. Not necessarily an object, but something you can't see. Something from within themselves. What people wouldn't dare do anywhere else, they succumb to here. Their darker nature gets the run of the motel room for a night, letting loose in a safe haven for strangers. They all think that, when they check out the next morning, they've just severed their impurities from the rest of themselves. Leaving it for me to wipe up. They go about their business like nothing happened, as if staying in a motel could cleanse their soul. That salvation came with a set of towels and a complimentary breath mint.

What it really does is defile my home. Taints these rooms until I can taste the bitter flavor in the air—the carpets drenched with every dirty deed done in there, the ceilings soiled with it. Believe it or not, I was pretty possessive of this place. Outside the window, I could hear those kids raping my rooms, molesting this motel. Once the night was over and all the alcohol was gone, they'd hop back into their cars, leaving behind a mess that would take a week for me to mop up—and none of them would ever think twice about what they'd done. They could drive away and never look back.

The second I laid down, I felt this lump running up the middle of the mattress. Tenants leave their junk behind all the time. Loose change, old magazines. Food from days ago, stinking up the whole room. You name it—and I've had to scrape it off. Never surprises me to find something stuffed under the bed. Weird sex toys. Spent prophylactics. But I felt like the Princess and the Pea, here—the bulge big enough to press against my back.

Reaching in between the mattress and the frame, the bed had swallowed my arm up to the elbow before I touched anything. I suddenly tapped at this tenderness I wasn't expecting to find. Something doughy. Soft and stiff at the same time. Didn't faze me, at first. I'd come across worse. Pricked my finger on a needle once—so I didn't flinch over this. I simply got a firm grip around whatever it was and pulled, figuring I was about to pull out some old pervert's paraphernalia. A dildo or something.

Funny how that arm slipped free from the mattress without a shoulder. Or a body. It just stopped. Nothing beyond her elbow. It was a woman's arm. You could tell by her painted fingernails. How her hand had gotten stuffed under the bed was beyond me. All I knew for sure was that she had one hell of a firm grip. Felt like it kept tightening around my hand, squeezing me harder. I couldn't tell if I was the one who wouldn't let go, or her. The air between our boxed palms heated up, getting me to sweat while she kept clammy. Shaking my hand, she greeted me by saying, *What this motel's been missing is a woman's touch.*

And I believed her. I knew she had to be right. How else could you explain something like that? Her skin held a tenderness that made me tremble. I can't even tell you the last time I'd touched something as soft as that. No blanket, no matter how fine the fabric, could compare to her hand.

When opportunity comes knocking, you answer—no matter how awkward it sounds. Right then, I realized I'd found a way in which to cut myself off from the Henley Road Motel for the rest of my life. *Envision your success and success will follow*. For me, the only vision I was getting was to burn this business down. I took an empty pillowcase and wrapped it around her elbow, knotting off the stump. Found a bottle of booze left in the parking lot, which I emptied over the end of her arm, dousing the linen in alcohol. Striking a match, I lit her like a torch—a perfect yellow flame budding up from the elbow.

We held hands, strolling from room to room. I used my father's skeleton key to quietly latch each door, while she was the key that unlocked the fire. Rubbed her stump across the paneling, the wood welcoming the flames. Nobody even noticed the blaze until they started suffocating. Laughter quickly curdled into coughing, each room turning into its own furnace full of high-school students. Heard enough hollering to recall those hatchlings from the front sign five years ago—each baby bird swallowing back more and more smoke, soot seeping into their lungs. A steady rhythm of fists began pounding against the doors, a cymbal crash of broken glass bursting through the windows. The sound of fire was everywhere, the phonetics of an inferno filling the open air.

I sat in the parking lot and followed the flames through each room, watching the bodies writhe behind the windows. With those kids still in their evening attire, looked to me like they were all dancing—the boys with their molten tuxedos, the girls in their scorched gowns. They partied until they dropped, one by one. Bet it was the best prom they'd ever had.

The entire motel was overcome by fire. There wasn't an inch of wood that wasn't burning, the blaze lifting off the rooftop and into the sky. From where I sat, I felt as if I was only a few steps away from the rising sun, the horizon now penetrating my parking lot. The heat was too much for my cheeks—the light so bright, I had to squint to look into it. But I watched the dawn blossom up from the Henley Road Motel, fed by the flesh of so many children that I believed the sun to be one big mass of burning bodies. Light was nothing but skin feeding flames. A day's worth of sun would run you the world's population, and then some.

I stayed there all night, watching the fire finally fade—sunset sinking in only after a couple hours. Sifting through the rooms, a layer of high-school kids now carpeted the floor. Their ashes were inseparable. Found my father where the office had been. I doubt he'd even gotten up from behind his desk, watching his television set as he fried.

The only relic of the motel left standing was the front sign. I took the woman's arm and slid it inside the hole where Posey had first snuck in, figuring that would be the safest place for her. I felt like I was in the Olympics or something, lighting the inaugural torch. She'd be there forever, mixing in with my pussycat's bones. I could come back for her whenever I wanted.

Morning was on its way, the real sun starting to peek out from the highway. Wouldn't be too long before someone drove by—some parent wondering why their son or daughter hadn't come home last night. I went ahead and picked out a new automobile from the lot, sitting behind the wheel like pulling someone else's skin over my bones. I chose Will Colby's car. It had been my first, so I felt akin to it—even if it was the most ragged one on the lot. Nobody'd recognize me in here, 'cause driving a different automobile was like slipping into a new identity. The engine purred at my back, like a cat rolling its throat. Felt like Posey was there with me, one way or another. I put that car into drive and shot straight down the highway, speeding into the sun just before it lifted off the ground. Drove straight into a solar flare and never looked back.

But the kicker is, what I found on the other side of the horizon was this. I did one big circle around the globe and came right back where I started. I drove just about everywhere—first heading west, then budging up north. Nothing ever felt real to me, not like my motel. I swear, there isn't anything in this world for a Henley. Just a road that bends back home.

An insurance check found me a couple years later. Took long enough to reach me, after running all over the country. I'd moved from one state to the next for almost a decade, hopping towns until there wasn't anywhere else I wanted to go. Just when I thought I'd found somewhere to settle, up walks this man in a suit looking for me. I couldn't believe it. My grandfather had taken out a policy on the family business ages ago. Just like a weed, no matter how many times I think I've pulled up the last of it, there are always enough roots left for this motel to sprout out of the ground again. For the next of kin. All this place ever needed was some new blood.

And here I am, all over again—providing. Emptied almost every vein I have for it—leaving me as dry as Route 52, here. I'll stand under the sign during the summer months, hiding inside the shade. Watching the road. Waiting. Sometimes, I'll get worked up when I think I see a car coming, only to realize it's nothing but the heat rising up from the asphalt, rippling through the air. If an automobile ever does head my way, I'll blink twice—just to make sure. And when I'm positive I'm not mistaking a mirage for another customer, I'll wait in place. Hold out long enough for the driver to wave back at me, pulling his attention off the road. If I hear a knock above my head, that arm signaling for me to let whatever animal it is that I found that morning go, I'll toss it at just the right moment. Cats need two yards' worth of time, fawns only need one. And depending on what I'm planting that day, I can harvest myself anything from a family of four, to a traveling salesman, or even just some truck driver. Doesn't matter to me. There's always at least one room available here. Stay as long as you want.

william colby

In sleep, the hollow knocking of someone's knuckles on the window sounds a lot like Shelly's limbs brushing up against the bathtub. Putting my ear near her inner thigh, I had heard the ocean from inside her torso—the sounds of the sea washing over her womb.

"You can't sleep here, sir," this police officer said, scanning through the inside of my new Honda Accord.

I woke up by the side of the highway, the rush of steady traffic sounding like water pouring into the tub. The highway patrolman was leaning over, peering in. After last night's accident, I figured it'd be best to leave my sedan behind. These kids must not worry over keeping their cars unlocked, let alone leaving their keys in the ignition. This one had been sitting at the far end of the motel's parking lot, the light from the street lamps just barely reaching its baby blue body. Once I was on the road again, the clock radio said it was close to two in the morning. For every pair of headlights that passed me, I saw four—the lack of sleep catching up with me.

Shelly had kept me awake all night. I'd decided to pull off the highway to take a quick nap, only to wake up the next morning to this officer's fist.

"I'm going to have to give you a ticket if you don't get moving." Had he studied the inside of the car closer, he would've found the blue and gold graduation tassel hanging from the rearview mirror and recognized the team colors of some local high school. He might've noticed the wilted corsage in the front seat, even the bumper sticker at the back warning everyone else on the road that I was a *Bitch On Wheels!* The only items that caught this patrolman's attention, however, were the coolers in the backseat. "You wouldn't happen to have any alcohol in there, would you?"

"No sir. Just food for the road."

"Lotta drunk drivers rolling around here, lately. Last night alone, we had about five different accidents."

Hungover or not, my skull was spinning. Felt as if I had a head full of water. Taking the palm of my hand, I tapped at the side of my temple—attempting to empty the trapped bathwater out through my ears. Shaking my head over to my shoulder, the pressure in my ear finally popped. I felt that warm trickle of water roll down the lobe. My equilibrium came back. The traffic didn't sound as distant as before, the hum of cars filling up the highway.

I realized we were running low on gas. The arrow on the meter was leaning toward the empty mark, dipping right into the red. We wouldn't make it to Florida if we didn't pull over soon.

Funny to think that the real meaning of the word *honeymoon* has nothing to do with love. While I was overseas, near Norway, I learned that the origin of the word had its roots in their history. I can't pronounce the word they had for it, but I remember what it meant. The husband-to-be would abduct his fiancée, hiding her from her family for months. When everyone else had given up on finding her, she would finally be his—the two of them returning as husband and wife. Talk about getting on your father-in-law's bad side.

All the girl can drink is this type of wine laced with honey, which is supposed to sweeten her period. Since it's believed that menstruation was linked to the lunar cycle, the groom feeds her this sugary cocktail for days leading up to the full moon. They'll wait to consummate their marriage until the sky is completely illuminated, the wife's monthly cycle paving out a pathway to heavenly pleasure for her husband. That's why pallolo maggots are called honeymoon worms. Their reproductive system is in phase with the moon, their sexual organs maturing in the lunar cycle's last quarter.

It's funny what you learn while you're out at sea. The most trivial bits of information become so important later down the road, acclimating to your rationale when you need to make sense out of something so numbing as this. Our honeymoon might not be perfect, Shelly—but I'm determined to make the most of it. This trip will be a testament to our love. There's a legacy to this land that we've become a part of. Our bloodline's bound to the ground now. I've planted my family along the road. I've plowed through the pavement, harrowing this highway with my car. I've tilled this entire interstate. It's yours. There isn't a stop along this freeway that isn't marked with a body part, a new batch of mile markers posted wherever we've pulled over. Whenever people drive through, they'll use you to guide them along—following your body from state to state. You've become the signpost for folks to hold their course, your arms and legs leading people home.

That's the way I want to remember you. I may not have been there when you needed me the most, but I'll make up for it by mapping out our marriage, inseminating the south with the seeds of our love.

This was destined to happen. Think back to how we found each other. We were just kids when we first met, the two of us colliding into one another on our bikes. I had been riding home, while you were coming the opposite way. The bike you were on was too big for you, your slender legs barely able to even reach the pedals. You had trouble keeping control over your direction, cutting across the road and back again. The closer I got to you, the less I paid attention to where I was heading—looking at your cropped hair instead, how it curled just under your ears. I could count the number of freckles spread across your nose, we were so close to each other. You turned toward my front tire, until our handlebars locked, sending the two of us forward. Our heads met in the clumsiest kiss ever. You gave me a bloody nose while you lost a tooth. We both fell, tumbling to the pavement. My knee hit the asphalt first, scraping its way over the road. Your shoe got caught in the spokes of my tire. Buried under our bikes, we both cried our eyes out—sniffling our way toward each other. Your cheeks were puffed and blushing, your eyes bloodshot and wet. I asked if you were okay. You nodded your head, saying your foot hurt. You asked me if I was okay, and I nodded back, saying my knee felt like it had fallen off. We helped each other up, limping home. We left our bikes by the side of the road, tangled together—while we propped our arms over each other's shoulders, wrapping ourselves together for the first time. Holding each other up.

Looking back now, I can't think of a better way to have met you.

northbound

florida

Well—gooo-oood morning, everybody. It's bright and early on a Thursday. Seven-fifteen by my watch. If any of you out there had some sense, you probably wouldn't be listening to me right now. You'd be sleeping in, for the love of God. But if my voice is reaching you out there in radio land—then rise and shine, Florida. It's going to be another hot day. The sun's already up and the temperature's itching to hit an all-time high—plateauing this afternoon somewhere around 90 degrees. Hope the air conditioner's working in your car, 'cause if you're anywhere near Interstate 79—you're in for a long haul, my friends. Traffic's looking pretty bad in the southbound lane, slowing things down from Gainesville on to Ocala. But don't take my word for it—I'm not out there. You are. Happy traveling, folks . . .

philip winters

The call came in two days ago. The telephone ruptured up in a ring, jogging me out of my sleep. Whatever time it was, it felt late. I was too deep into my sleep for it to be early. The clock seemed distant, the numbers out of focus for me.

"Philip Winters? It's John Thompson. From the station. Officer Thompson. You remember me?"

There was a pause. The crackle of our weak connection pricked at my ear.

"Listen. I don't know how to prepare you for this, so I'm just going to come out and say it. We found your son. Thirty miles south from your house, just off Route 27."

"Kevin?" His name rubbed my Adam's apple up and down my neck, like a slice of butter melting in a frying pan. It was the first time I'd said his name out loud in months.

"You know where the swamp starts running alongside the road? Your van, it's been down there for I don't know how long.

We called in a towtruck to drag it out. They should be here in less than thirty minutes."

Did he have his inhaler with him? I'd need to bring one with me, I thought. Just in case he'd lost his somewhere along the way. No matter how many extras we stocked up on, stashing them in his pants pockets, slipping them in his knapsack—he'd always lose his inhaler.

It would've been easy enough to have just laid down again and gone back to sleep, waking up the next morning and believing that it had all been a dream. I'd been imagining this moment for five years now: Picking up the phone, listening to the officer on the other end, wondering where I'd have to go to pick Kevin up. But I'd dreamed up better moments than that. I think I liked my imaginary version better: An officer came to the door and drove me to the station to pick him up. Other times—they'd bring him back home to me, a blanket wrapped around his shoulders, shivering cold.

It was easier to focus on the clock now. It was three in the morning. The ripe pink minutes twisted and rolled over top of each other as three-fifteen passed, three-thirty. Kevin might not even recognize me anymore. His own fattened father. Time had tugged on my stomach. My belly had finally slackened away from the rest of me, a slight paunch seeping out from my waist. I remembered how he used to lay across the stretch of my chest in that very bed, the two of us sprawled out together—father cushioning four-year-old son. We'd fall asleep like that, Kevin's head pinned into place by my bare chin, his blond hair slipping down the neck of my shirt.

This soreness seeped into my chest. It's been coming and going all the time now—this strain around my lungs, as if my ribs were tightening around them. Reaching over to my nightstand, I dipped into the drawer and fished out this sliver of plastic that fit firmly in my palm. Printed across its side, the inhaler read: KEVIN WINTERS, ISSUED MARCH 20, 1995, REFILL UNDER DOCTOR'S NOTICE ONLY. Squeezing it, I got this gust of medicated air in my mouth, washing away the taste of sleep. The draft rushed down my throat, the swell of wet metal collecting inside my lungs. Breathing came easier now. My chest felt revived.

Ever since my wife, Delila, left, our house has had to pick up after itself—leaving enough dust to clump up wherever I don't step anymore. It had always been Kevin's job to wrangle up the dust bunnies, at least when he'd been five—before we knew how heavy his asthma really was. The whole family made a game out of our house cleaning. Edey was too young to play along, always attempting to eat the fuzz clusters like they were candy. Delila would holster Edey in at her hip while vacuuming with her free hand, the two of them letting out a low drone along with the engine's whirring—a domestic Indian chant.

"What do I do with the bunnies now, Dad?" Kevin had asked, holding up a handful of dust and hair.

"We take them over to the . . . bunny-eating elephant!"

"N*ooo*!" *Gasp.* "Not the bunny-eating." *Gasp.* "Elephant!"

"Here he comes!" Delila yelled over the vacuum, as Edey roared along with the engine. The funnel snorted the hair and dust right up from Kevin's hand, his skin clogging the current of air. He'd shout as the vacuum's nozzle hissed in the air from the edges of his hand.

Now those dust bunnies have overtaken the entire house. They've been breeding, their numbers rapidly multiplying. Whenever I walk through the hallway, the current of air behind me will pick up the lighter clumps from the floor—as if they were hopping after me in the wake of my feet. I've herded my own litter of inanimate pets, formed from the fragments of my shed skin. They've sewed themselves together with my thinning hair, bred from the scraps of my body.

The only room in the house that's kept its composure has been Kevin's. Whenever I walk past his door, I'll stop long enough to look inside. See if anything's changed. It has stayed exactly the same since Kevin left. Nothing has been moved or picked up. The same sheets are still on his bed, the pillowcase retaining the slightest scent of my son.

Behind the desk, I keep getting caught in the window overlooking our backyard. That morning, after the call, the sun was still another hour away from rising. Miles' worth of forest stood at the end of our property, probably the only woods in all of Florida that suburban corpulence had left alone. Our neighborhood still ends with our house. There's enough marsh hiding under those trees to swallow our whole block. It's a shock that the ground is sturdy enough to hold up the woods in the first place. Our house had come cheap because of all that swampland. When Kevin was twelve, he and a friend of his, Spencer Partridge, slipped through that veil of trees—only to stumble out a half hour later, completely drenched, their arms reaching out from their sides. I found the first leech on his cheek, another dangling from his chin. One had cuddled up behind his earlobe. Their arms were covered, the leeches swinging from their skin like ornaments hung off a Christmas tree. Kevin couldn't stop hollering. His throat only hocked up half of his voice—the other half as good as gravel, coarse and hissing.

"Kevin, where's your inhaler?"

"Dropped it." *Gasp.* "In the." *Gasp.* "Water." The color was draining from his cheeks. His lips were blue. The air wasn't reaching his lungs anymore. The leeches curled their tails up as the blood sunk from his skin.

"Kevin," I had to hold him by the shoulders to keep him focused. "Where's your extra inhaler?"

"Bba. Ba . . ."

"In the bathroom?"

The irises in his eyes drifted into his skull, leaving behind a wake of white. He folded into my arms, his breathing as shallow as puddles, the air barely there. I had to run into the house, find his spare inhaler—I ran back out and slipped it in between Kevin's lips. I remember hearing the click of plastic against his teeth. The blood was finally coming back to his face then, blushing across his cheeks like storm clouds forming over his flesh. The leeches gorged themselves on the sudden swell, plumping up all over again.

When everyone recommended Delila and I join the other families in suffering together, *to release this pain that I wouldn't let go of*, to acknowledge this grief that had gripped onto our hearts, this fist in our chest dragging everyone else to these meetings for victims of uncertainty, where people actually said things like, *the not-knowing is the hardest part, actually making the decision to move on, to let go, to accept the fact that our son is probably dead so we can finally just get on with the rest of our lives,* to know that fathers actually said these things, men who I'd known for years, who'd thrown barbecues in their backyards while our kids ran around—the woods just a few feet away the whole time, seeing them cry over their children now . . . Empathy was asking me to relate with these people. Grief was pleading with me to admit my child was never walking through our front door again.

For the one-year anniversary of our loss, all five families gathered out in the street. The Partridges, the Clarks, the Wilsons, and the Raymonds all collected in the cul-de-sac. Candles in hand, the road lit up with these parents' tear-ridden faces. Delila had taken Edey outside to join the group. They shared a candle together, Edey's fingers pinching at the melted wax that had dripped onto her hand.

I stood inside by the window, the curtain peeled back enough to watch. To hear the sobbing start. The rest of the neighborhood was willing to give in after just one year. They all lacked the spine to endure an empty bedroom, an empty place at the dinner table—needing to whimper among each other, when the problem should've been kept at home. With family. Not among these people. Not among strangers.

I focused on Edey, her cheeks streaked—the tears glistening in the candlelight. My temper suddenly flared, aware of the fact that my daughter was slipping into the same mind-set as the rest of the block. Storming out the front door, I crossed over the lawn. "Edey, come here. Come back inside with Daddy."

"Phil. Don't." Delila backed up a couple of steps, shielding herself within the crowd.

"Phil, . . ." Paul Clark started in, his calm voice always saddling him at the forefront of the group. "Why don't you just stay out here with us? It would mean a lot to everybody."

"Come with me, honey. I want you inside."

"Let Edey stay, Phil." Delila kept stepping back, weaving through the crowd.

Paul Clark placed his free hand on my shoulder, trying to hold me back. "Phil, please."

I slapped Paul's hand that had been holding the candle, snubbing the flame directly across his cheek. The light snuffed out in Paul's skin, sizzling into darkness. He let out a yell, grabbing for his face.

The crowd split into couples, all the neighbors stepping back. I kept turning, searching for Edey in there. "Delila. Back inside. Come on."

"You're ruining this for the whole neighborhood, you know

that?" It was Frank Partridge's wife. She had hissed at me from behind her candle—the wick flickering with her breath. "The neighborhood's been ruined for a year now, because you treat this block like a God-damned mortuary!"

"Your son was the one driving." Wendy Raymond spoke up, my own next-door neighbor. Her face was stiff, the muscles not working, frozen over from so much crying that they couldn't maneuver her mouth anymore.

"Wendy?" Finally Delila spoke up, her voice squeezed.

"I'm sorry, Delila. *But listen to him!* Look at what he's done to our neighborhood!"

Paul Clark grabbed me from behind, wrapping his arms around my chest. I only had to lean over to send Paul toppling onto the pavement, hitting his head hard on the road. That's when the other husbands dove in. The candles the men had been holding were rolling over the road, the lights flickering out. Fists hailed in, the dark obscuring who was actually hitting whom—but it's safe to say the whole block was getting their fair share of me.

Everybody walked back home. Doors slammed shut, lights turned off—until the whole block was quiet again. Candle wax covered the pavement, clotting up around my body like a translucent chalk-circle.

Delila had taken Edey back inside, packing up a suitcase for the two of them. I stayed out in the street, lying there. I heard her walk out into the garage, start up her car. I stayed in my place, slumped over in the cul-de-sac. This neighborhood had become a graveyard for families. Each home was its own tombstone.

In Kevin's room, on top of his desk, the lamp light spread over six unused inhalers, all of them dating back five years. I stuffed each one into a different pocket. Before I turned the light off, I caught one last glance at the woods outside. I didn't need to sift through those trees in hopes of finding my son anymore. I could stare right into that forest and not even flinch. Because as morning thawed out the nighttime sky, I could just barely make out a chasm within the woods, the trees dividing evenly apart for a long stretch of road.

Route 27 was only a half hour away.

The morning traffic had another hour before hemorrhaging over the highway, the road still bare of automobiles. The drive was such a lull, easing me off even deeper into drowsiness. My head leaned in with every bend on the highway, my body drifting with the turns. I'd driven down this road enough times to know where it sloped and curled, the contours of the asphalt practically ingrained into my bones. I could almost close my eyes and ride.

The trees along the road had grown right up to the ditch, the forest curling over the asphalt. I still needed my high beams to see where I was steering, shrouded from what little light there was creeping over Florida at four in the morning. The sun had slowly begun to seep in through the tunnel of trees. The fog was lit in dense streaks of orange, settling along the pavement, as if the forest had been carved in two—dawn bleeding up from the bog.

After another turn, I entered into a tableau of police cars and firetrucks. A network of blue and red veins began winding through the fog, the flash of police lights solidified within the muggy atmosphere. The silhouette of an officer passed through a pair of headlights, walking up the road. From his hand, a burst of burning pink light spurted out, then another. He was laying down flares along the road's shoulder, constricting the eventual two-lane traffic into a one-lane clot—as if he were tying off someone's arm to squeeze up a vein.

I could barely see the marsh nuzzling up to the road. The long stretch of canal divided into halves by the highway, extending out through the woods. The trees thinned out around here, the swamp deeper in these parts than most other spots. The water probably reached down some twenty feet. Depending on where you measured, I bet you could've found a block's worth of houses hidden under the marsh—the lost neighborhood of Atlantis all swallowed up by that swamp.

Switching off my headlights, the red and blue beams from the police cars took over the dark, striking the sparse number of trees. A police officer hailed in the towtruck, motioning for the driver to pull up to the water's edge. It was finally time to cut into this marsh's belly, dredge up Kevin. Couldn't help but have my mind wander back as far as my first visit to the maternity ward, remembering when I saw him for the first time. Kevin rested in his own cot, lined up in a winding row of other babies—all of them squirming blindly, their parents clumping together on the other side of this window, sifting through the bodies to find their own child.

I had an old knapsack of Kevin's in my hand. I rolled it up and stuffed it under my armpit. I looked both ways before crossing the road. No one was around. No cars, none of the other families. Just me and the police. The strong odor of sulfur burned below my nose as I passed through the long line of flares, the pink streak of pure fire licking the pavement. None of the officers seemed to notice me. I walked among them as if I wasn't there, a ghost to those who recognized me.

The water reached into a wad of fog a few yards off. If it were clearer, I could've found the woods looming just over the marsh. Maybe even my own house off in the distance, spotting Kevin's window from the other side of the swamp. Tucked onto the shore was a little two-man mud-skipper, a couple fishing poles hanging out over its stern. A bucket of night crawlers sat at the bow, the squirm of worms filling in the silence. Their bodies wriggled into numbers for me, the date of every day Kevin had been gone forming one after another. June 25, 26, 27, 28, 29 . . . On and on and on, tallying up five years. One thousand, eight hundred and twenty-five days total.

An old man was standing with an officer farther down the shore. He pointed toward the water, his arm unable to extend out completely—either from arthritis or shock. With his hands, he made out a rectangular shape in the air, as if to sketch a diagram of something boxy, large—then pointed back toward the marsh again. He nodded his head, his chin signaling for the officer to look out at the water. To find *it*, just below the surface.

This was the fisherman I had to thank for finding my son, some stodgy old coot who probably fried up snapping turtles when nothing else was biting. I knew what had happened without even needing to ask. This fisherman had cast off his line over the van, the hook snagging onto the rear bumper. Probably thought he had caught himself a live one, from the struggle he'd gone through. His wishbone shoulders had to have been close to cracking in half after a minute's worth of trying to reel that van in. Before giving up, the old man probably leaned over the edge of his trawler to see just what it was that he had hooked—thinking, he'd find a branch below the surface, or a tire protruding out from the mud.

But when he spotted that algae-laced outline of a 1989 Ford van a few feet underneath his boat, buried under enough sediment to emanate the impression of a sunken ship—that old man's jaw must have just dropped. The blue and white paint job had to have barely been there, years worth of silt sanding it off. The license plate must've been obscured by his own reflection, his head eclipsing the morning light from seeing the numbers.

The towtruck backed, parting the group of men in half. A droning pulse from the cab rung out as it reversed. The mud on the shore spread open under the truck's weight, like lips wrapping over the tires, sucking the rubber into the ground's mouth. Two separate tracks stretched from the road on down to the marsh. Those brown lips now peeled back to reveal gritted teeth, the tires imprinting their design along the coast. The rear wheels rolled right into the water, the bumper dipping under the surface, disappearing below. The winch now dangled directly over the marsh, the hook rocking on its chain like a clock's pendulum ticking down the seconds before dropping into the water.

They were going fishing for my son, casting the towtruck's line in as if Kevin would bite its bait. The hook would catch the van and reel it back onto dry land after all these years.

I rubbed my thumbs over the knuckles of each finger, trying to squeeze the circulation back into my hands. The cold hung in the air, my breath drifting out of my mouth in visible wisps of mist—as if I was adding my oxygen to the fog. The morning's haze must've been a collection of every man's breath, the air scuttling up our throats and hanging over the marsh. It loomed inches above the surface, taunting those who drowned. I knew it, understood how that cloud of dense air must have looked like cotton candy to everyone on the other side of the water. I felt this twinge of bitterness at the fog, wondering how easy it would have been for one of those kids to have reached out from the swamp, tearing off just the slightest piece of mist and bringing it back down into the water. They could've eaten from the atmosphere until they were all able to breathe again. Those kids could have survived off of that orchard of air. It hung so close to the surface—if one of them could've just reached it, they might have been able to rip off a breath for everyone below.

A chink of chain sounded, the pulley system rigged onto the back of the towtruck spitting out its line. The rattle of metal hushed over as soon as the chain dipped under the surface, the noise swallowed with each link. I watched the driver as he lowered the winch. He looked as if he had not slept for days. His cheeks were hollowed down with tire grease, his expressionless face following the thick iron hook into the water. He probably had no idea what he was about to bring back up.

A diver from the fire department was slipping on the last fin of his wet suit, his body wrapped in black rubber. The only visible piece of the man that I could find was his face, the upper portion of his cheeks bulging up from the rest of his skull. His lips puckered under the pressure of such a tight fit. He had strapped on his diving mask before I could make out his eyes. I wanted to know who this man was, what he looked like—just to see who I was allowing to save my son. He waddled out backward into the swamp, the fins on his feet slapping down loudly against the shore, kicking up mud onto his knees. The rest of the firemen and police officers crowded around the coast, letting the mud suck in their shoes. The entire group watched their man slip off into the swamp. Once he was up to his waist in the water, he gave a thumbs-up to everyone and leaned back against the surface, tipping over into the marsh. He disappeared, then bobbed back up. A mist of wet air sprayed out from his mouth.

"Cold enough?" one of the officers called out.

"Christ, man. Thought this was Florida."

"Where's the hook?"

"Head out to the left a little. Just a few feet back."

"Christ, it's so sloppy out here. I can't find nothing."

"It's a van, Rob. Even you could find it." A chuckle came up from the line of officers.

Not for the last five years, they couldn't.

With a heavy inhale, the diver disappeared under the surface again—his wake radiating outward in a series of perfect circles. A line of bubbles lifted up from the water, following one another. I counted them all. Four. Ten. July fifteenth. July twentieth. September thirtieth.

Kevin had first lost his inhaler out here, somewhere. This swamp had been hungering over my son's lungs for all of his life, almost—wanting to squeeze what little air Kevin needed to breathe and take over that hollow. He'd say it was destiny that he ended up out here, down below.

I remembered how his lips had purpled over before even walking out the front door.

"I'm heading out now . . ." *Gasp.* "Bye, guys."

Delila had looked over to me—wanting to make sure I'd heard it, too. I pulled up from the television without saying anything, staring at Kevin.

"Oh, come on . . ." He started, swallowing the air in, hoping to avoid the choking noise his throat made when it started clenching. "I'm fine. I have my inhaler with me."

"Who's driving?"

"Me."

"Oh, you think so?"

"Dad . . ." *Gasp.*

"Get one of the other kids to drive."

"But we . . ." *Gasp.* The air was breaking up more frequently now, his breaths shallower with each inhale. "But we're the only ones . . ." *Gasp.* "Only ones with a car big enough for . . ." *Gasp.* "Everybody!"

"Take separate cars."

"But I promised I'd take everyone!"

"I don't want you driving. Listen to yourself."

"But I . . ." *Gasp*. "I already said I would. Everybody's depending on me." His lips lost their pink.

"I'll drive you guys. How about that?"

"No!" *Gasp. Gasp*. "You said I could drive tonight, Dad. So . . ." *Gasp*. "I'm going to . . . drive."

Delila stood up from the couch. "Calm down, Kevin. You're only making your asthma worse—"

"Shut up about my . . ." *Gasp*. "Fucking asthma!" Kevin stormed outside, the door swinging behind him.

"Kevin! Don't talk that way to your mother." I followed him outside, walking right into a cluster of kids. Josh Raymond, Tamara Clark, Mandy Wilson, and Spence Partridge were all in our driveway, waiting to get into the car. Kevin had pulled back the sliding door at the side of the van, opening up the hollow for the others to crawl in. There was a moment of hesitation from the group. None of them knew what to do.

"Let's go," Kevin said, opening up the driver's-side door.

"Where are you going?" I asked.

"What? You going to . . . follow us?"

"You're not taking out my van if I don't know where you're taking it."

"I'm going to Little League tryouts, Dad . . . How about that? Are you happy now?" He had slipped the keys into the ignition already, turning the car over. Kevin put the van into reverse, pulling out of the driveway so fast the tires skidded over the road. They turned at the end of the block and disappeared from sight, the hum of the engine thinning out into the air.

One o'clock passed—an hour after Kevin's curfew. If he had ever been late coming home before, he always called. Edey had gone to sleep hours ago, the lights turned off all throughout the house. The living room was cast in a blue glow from the television set, all the colors losing their properties for a more aquamarine tint—as if the entire living room had been immersed in water. I weighed myself down at the bottom, my own skin flushed into a cold bloodless hue.

The phone finally rang at two. I tried scooping up the receiver on the second ring, running up the stairs by the third, accidentally knocking the phone off of its cradle.

"Hello?"

"Phil?"

"Yeah?"

"It's Paul Clark. Tamara wouldn't happen to be there, would she? She hasn't come home yet. I'll pick her up if Kevin's too tired to drop her off—"

"She's not here, Paul. They're still out."

"You're kidding me. It's after two in the morning."

"I'll tell her to go right home if she comes over, okay?"

"Where was Kevin taking her, anyway?"

When their names were called for roll the next morning at school, none of the neighborhood's children answered. Their desks sat empty for the rest of the week, like gaping wounds within the classroom. After a month had passed, their chairs scarred over with the bodies of other students.

Two months later, the school had asked all of the parents to come clean out their children's lockers. When I picked through Kevin's books and pictures, I found a half dozen inhalers scattered about the bottom. He had tied a shoelace around his most recent prescription. I lifted the necklace, slipping the inhaler around my neck. The shoelace was so long the mouthpiece swung at my belly—a plastic pendulum scraping my navel.

The bell rang, the classroom doors bursting open. The hallway was overflowing with kids, like a twisted spigot releasing a deluge of water throughout the school. Students were heading to their lockers, the spin of their dial's combinations sending an internal murmur of metal through the row of consolidated closets. I stood where Kevin would have been right then, if he were at school—this forty-year-old man hovering over the heads of a hundred sixteen-year-olds.

"Mr. Winters?"

Turning around, I found myself facing one of Kevin's friends, suddenly realizing I was still wearing his inhaler around my neck. "Hello, Carrie."

"I'm sorry, sir. I didn't mean to—"

"How are your parents doing?"

"My parents? Fine. They're fine."

"That's good."

A warning bell rang. "Do you think you'll need me to baby-sit for you guys anytime soon? I haven't seen Edey for like, forever."

"I don't think so, Carrie. We'll call you if we decide to ever go out again."

"Okay. Thanks."

She leaned back into the passing current of students, quickly disappearing inside the flow of peach-skinned, pink-lipped boys and girls. The flood of teenagers thinned itself down to the latecomers, drifting off to class—until I was all alone in the hall again. Kevin's locker was the only one still open, the door exposing his sophomore year to me for the first time. Pictures of Tamara were stuck to the inside of the door, a photo of Edey as a baby below it.

It hit me swiftly—this weight in my chest. I first thought to look around to see who had hit me, what had struck me. But the burden was inside, tugging on my lungs so much, it burned to breathe. My throat began to tighten. A sob lumped up into my Adam's apple. I swallowed it back down before the sound could reach my mouth.

My hand tangled around the shoelace around my neck, my fingers sliding right over the inhaler at my waist. I brought it to my lips, depressing the medicated air into my mouth. There was a shift within my lungs. I could breathe easier now, the strain on my ribs relenting. All it took was a rush of Kevin's medicine to cleanse me of any remorse. It swept up all the ill feeling inside of me, like a passing wind picking up dead leaves. I had finally found a way in which to push through the pain, something to help me through the next five years.

"We're hooked," the diver called out, floating over the surface of the water. "Start reeling her in."

The towtruck driver nodded, nearly slipping in the mud. Flipping the winch at the rear of the truck, the engine kicked into gear. The chain jittered in the water. A faint tinkle of metal began behind the men's backs, running past their shoulders. After hacking up a pipeful of exhaust, the crank reversed its track, pulling the slack back in from the swamp. The loose chain rose up from below the water, the links losing their grip on the marsh. The wobble within the line quickly tightened as the winch kept spinning, the chain now pinched between the truck and swamp.

As soon as the line lost its laxness, the engine seized. The winch's speed dropped to a crawl, the chain slowly looping around the crank. The towtruck now had to deal with the bulk below the water, attempting to tug the van up from beneath five years' worth of sediment.

I could understand that strain. I knew how it felt to lose one's grip on their family, that weakening in the joints. Every link just wants to split apart.

I stood on the shore, the tight line shifting abruptly over the surface. The ruptured water lapped at my feet in a faint wake—

the surface reverberating in a low current of waves, as if the swamp was giving sound to its struggle. The weight from the water was pulling the towtruck backward, the tires skidding through the mud toward the shore. It looked as if the swamp was winning, actually dragging the vehicle closer to the water. The driver turned his head in every direction, looking around helplessly—hoping to find something that his truck could hold on to.

"Whoa, whoa, whoa . . ." He leaned against the truck's side—thinking if he pushed with the winch, he might be able to keep the wheels from drifting down any farther. When his feet had skidded through enough mud for his heels to reach the water's edge, he finally flipped off the engine. The crank halted, the chain loosening again. The slack spilled back into the water with a wet *plop*, disappearing below the surface. The rattle of the engine dissipated into the early morning, the air calming itself all over.

"What happened?" the diver called. All the officers turned to the driver.

"Look." He pointed toward the tire treads farther up the shore, mapping out where the towtruck had been parked when the winch first got cranking. "Ever hear of a towtruck coming to tow another towtruck? The van's down too deep, I can't pull it up."

Looking out into the water, I tried following the chain link for link—to see if I could find the apparition of the van down below. Squinting, I could just barely make out its ghostly green aura settled within the swamp.

A couple of officers ambled back from the forest, their hands full of branches, soggy logs. They tucked the wood in front of the towtruck's rear tires, jamming a pyramid of rotten kindling between the rubber and mud. The squish went everywhere, brown streaks lashing out at the officers, a high-pitched squirt spurting up from the slush. Their uniforms were spackled brown.

The more puddles they put on, dressing themselves up in dirt, the younger they all looked. They wore freckles of grit on their cheeks, their hair caked down with brown water. Sweat was mingling in with their uniforms now, the day's humidity starting to seep into the air. I looked out into the woods and saw the morning sun reaching closer toward the horizon. Light had almost pried past these trees. A few minutes more and the swamp would be illuminated.

Dozens of footprints now dug down into the ground, the entire shoreline sprinkled with these hollow pockmarks of boots and shoes. The driver flicked the lever for a second time, the engine instantly heaving. It yanked the chain back out of the water, as if to catch the swamp by surprise. The engine seized within a second, the slack eaten immediately. The truck jolted, leaping backward onto its new wooden brakes. I could hear the wood warping as the tires pressed against them—this high intonation of stretching lumber, knots gripped into fists.

Once the logs had nearly sunk under the mud, burrowing into the earth completely, the truck stopped drifting. It stood on its haunches, the winch finally working in the right direction, cranking the chain back around. The water was parting, the surface peeling back to reveal a large metal frame.

At first the van looked like nothing more than a brown shadow, as if a cross section of the marsh's floor was rising up to the open air as it lifted toward the surface. Layer upon layer of mud pared free, the silt scalped from the van's exterior. What enamel was still intact on the metal looked like bone released from a blanket of its own dead skin, the exposed white and blue veneer calling up the image of a waterlogged skull—its eye sockets encased with murk-ridden windows, muck trapped behind the green tinted glass. Flakes of paint scattered out into the water, rust fluttering through a cloud of mud. Years worth of stillness had been cut completely, the fragile van incapable of keeping its coat of color on its own body. One slight shift was all it took to disintegrate, the ascent dispersing the van's rotten paint job back into the water.

The first thing to follow the chain up through the swamp's surface was the rear bumper, all rusted and soft underneath the hook. I was surprised it hadn't simply let go of the van, the sliver of old metal flinging up from the water and crashing onto the shore. But it held on, not wanting to let go—as a dog struggles against its owner's leash, its legs locked, dragged across the ground.

The license plate broke through the water next, the letters and numbers fading over Florida's chipped sunshine. I had forgotten that the state's plates looked different back then. They had changed since Kevin disappeared. People drive around with flamingos on the rears of their cars now. But there was the sun, a flaking orange dollop creeping out from the swamp—just as if it had been five years since it had last risen over Boca Raton.

All the officers and firemen huddled around the shore, stepping up to their ankles in water. No one cared about how wet they were anymore. They were finally seeing what they had come for, a mystery dissolving before their very eyes. A dozen men kept staring quietly at that chain, watching the van lurch out of the marsh.

The winch was close to snapping. Each link looked as if it could give in and break. The engine sounded as if it was screaming behind a locked jaw, the high-pitched cry leaking out through gritted teeth. All other sounds were washed away. Nothing could be heard, the towtruck spreading a layer of racket over everything else.

But I could hear Delila. Her voice crept into my ears, slipping right past the engine. She was humming Kevin's first lullaby. I heard it over the marsh, recalling the night she'd first returned home from the hospital. She had Kevin in her arms, pacing the room back and forth, her singing soothing our son off to sleep. I had been standing at the door, watching the two of them.

"What are you singing?"

"Nothing. Just something my mother used to sing to me. You want to hold him?" She held Kevin out to me, his body bundled in a soft blue blanket.

I smiled, watching the van uproot itself from the swamp—its wheels wobbling its body back onto shore.

"Yeah. Let me hold him."

As the van pulled up from the marsh, the swamp reconfigured itself. The water hesitated before letting go of the car, like lips on a lollipop as it slides out from the mouth. Once the front fender passed through the surface, the brown muck leveled with the tires, gripping on to whatever it could. The rear of the van was slowly inching onto dry land, the shore welcoming the back two tires onto earth again. They teetered on their own axles as a baby takes its first step. The towtruck stood patiently farther up the incline, the winch outstretched like a parent's open arms.

The van lunged onto the shore, its tires nearly folding under its own weight. The axles were as good as soggy sponge cake, held together solely by the impression of how solid the van used to be. Moss and algae clung to its exterior, the green afterbirth of the swamp glistening in the air. Water continued to flow, seeping out through rusted cracks—the trickle of a dozen spouts sounding out in a series of open faucets. It all dribbled down the van's sides, heading back into the swamp.

The van looked as if it was about to pop, its swollen belly bulging—its body developing a pearlike dimension. The roof had sunk in on itself, the sides first warping inward at the top, then sagging farther down toward the bottom.

An officer took a deep breath, gripping the handle of the back door. The metal collapsed right inside his palm. The handle tore off with one tug, a spout of water spraying through the fresh pair of holes it left.

"Get the crowbar."

Once he'd been obliged, he rammed the rod through the slit of the back door. The officer leaned in and the door folded with a soft, wet screech. A spring of water pelted out from the crack, the flow intensifying the harder the officer wedged the crowbar in.

"Stand back. The dam's gonna break."

The door buckled on its hinges before flinging wide open, the rest of the swamp rushing onto the shore. A tidal wave of rusted water toppled over the officers. The trapped marsh spread over everyone's feet, running up our legs as if our bodies had become bulkheads. The tail end of the drift was thicker than the initial deluge, a basin of mud pouring out from the floor. Within this sludge, an assortment of limp fish came spilling out. Eels glided off of the bumper, slapping the puddles below.

I didn't turn from the van. I watched the water pour out to the last trickle—the level dropping from the ceiling, passing below the seats, thinning down to the floor of the car. From where I stood, all I could see were the silhouettes of seats. Shadows of still figures were sitting in them. Nothing was moving. I could make out the heads and shoulders of the people inside—but nobody shifted toward the open door; they remained motionless.

As if on call, the sun finally pried through the woods. What dimness had hung over the forest dissolved, the morning's first light striking the algae-layered windshield. A green glow was cast across every surface inside the van. The seats, the inner walls, the ceiling, the floor—everything glistened with a wet sheen. Seat belts dangled, dripping water. A slight bubbling sound rattled through the entire cavity—as if air was lifting up from under a web of moss, pitter-pattering in a light drizzle.

The children were in their seats. Heads leaned over to the side awkwardly, as if they were all dozing off during a long ride. Losing the pressure of water all around them left their skeletons aimless, the bones unable to hold up their bodies on their own. The jaws that were still intact swung down to the neck. Others didn't have jaws at all—the crescent bone had dropped into their laps, tangled in with their pelvises. One skeleton had collapsed against the van's wall (Spence?), slouched over on its shoulder. I couldn't tell who was who. Their clothes had disintegrated around their bodies, mere remnants of shirts and pants clinging to shreds of gray skin. Hair had gone headless, peeling free and mingling in with the mud along the floor, a tide of fibers spilling out the back door. Their bodies had been washed away.

Looking as if you belong is just a matter of conviction. Act as if you're supposed to be there and no one even questions you. These officers were focused on the rear of the van, beginning to sift for remnants through the sediment along the floor, while I walked right up to the driver's-side door, drawing no attention to myself from anyone. The window was wrapped in algae, shielding the inside completely. Gently prying open the door, a quick flush of trapped water dropped onto my shirt.

Kevin nearly toppled onto me. His seat belt snagged his chest, hooking into his rib cage before he could tumble over. Kevin's head fell forward, the neck snapping, his skull dropping. It landed directly into the cup of my hands. I caught my son, the weight of my boy's head filling my palms.

"He's heavy, isn't he?" Delila had asked.

I remembered the weight of my baby, how it felt to hold Kevin for the first time.

"He's going to grow up to be a big boy. *Yeah, yeah . . .*" I cooed toward Kevin. Drool gurgled up from his lips. Water that had been trapped in his skull trickled out from his jaw, seeping through my fingers, collecting at my wrists, dripping off to the ground. Kevin's mouth was propped open, a sparse row of teeth lining his jaw. The air inside was stagnant, nothing moving in or out. He wasn't breathing, his breath trapped. A streak of panic seized me, wondering what I could do to revive him. I fished through my jacket pocket, pulling out the first inhaler my fingers wrapped around. I slipped the mouthpiece into Kevin's mouth, the clack of plastic tapping against his loose teeth. I squeezed the inhaler tightly, a hiss of medicated air whisking into the hollow. The rush brushed past algae, sending a mist of green water spurting out the back of his skull. The jaw loosened, the waterlogged tendons releasing Kevin's mouth.

Route 27 wriggled up as far as Lake Wales, where I would switch over to Route 4. From there, I could connect with Interstate 95 in about an hour, leading all the way up to South Carolina. Delila had taken Edey up to Sumter, renting an apartment of her own. Flipping the ignition to the car, I realized it was finally time to bring Kevin home.

the mourning glory group

Well, I see our numbers are dwindling a bit. But that's okay. Only makes our circle tighter, right? Fewer chairs for us to fold up at the end of the night.

Seriously, we're going to have to expect people to leave. We have to accept the fact that this group is a temporary form of therapy, not a permanent one. The grieving process is different for all of us. Even if the sun rises at the same time for everyone here, we wake up when we need to—whenever we're ready to see the morning's light. Until then, we're fortunate enough to have this. To have each other. None of us need to feel like we're going through this ordeal alone. That there are others who we can share our grief with—and eventually, when we're ready to open our eyes, we can wake up from this experience and start a brand-new day. One without remorse. But a fresh outlook on life. *Your* life. We can finally wipe away the crust of misery from our eyes, allowing ourselves to see what we've been blind to for all these years.

I know that's what I want. What *we* all should want. Isn't it, guys?

Why else would we be here?

Margaret. Why are you here? I mean, I know why you signed up for the group. We all know why you and Paul come here every week. But I want to know what *compels* you to come. What inside you tells you to get into your car and drive to this elementary school every Wednesday night, walk through the very halls your daughter had skipped down to get to her class nearly a decade ago, and sit in this gym where she probably learned how to toss her first foul shot?

Are you still looking for Tamara? Do you think you'll find her here? Maybe come across a picture she drew back in kindergarten, forgotten for the last five years, still taped to the art room wall? Do you think that would bring her home?

If that's what drags you here, Margaret, week after week, then you're only being lured deeper into your own remorse. You're being tempted by a false hope of getting Tamara back, a carrot dangling over your head, leading you along a *path of pain*. And the longer you stray away like this, the further off you're going to be from getting on with your own life.

That's the funny thing about sorrow, guys. It's like fire. It grows the longer your hope stokes it. It's feeding off your grief, as we speak. Right now. The love for your children is fuel for those flames, folks. And the pain's going to keep burning through until there's nothing left in your heart to preserve it—leaving the life you had before your misfortune in a heap of ashes, your very soul in cinders.

So what did we agree was that first step back toward ourselves? How do we pull off this *path of pain*?

Anyone? Somebody said it last week. I know you remember.

Paul. Remember what you told the group?

How could the rest of us forget? Right, guys? Remember when we first gathered last Wednesday, how we all noticed Margaret's black eye right off the bat? Took us by surprise, didn't it? I know I wasn't expecting to see that bruise.

It took courage for Paul to admit how he's been treating Margaret at home. How his remorse was affecting the way he acted around his wife. You see, when Paul is in his house, he doesn't notice the people still surrounding him. He latches on to the mementos of Tamara. All her pictures, her records, her stuffed animals. These items give his hope something to hold on to. He chooses not to embrace the functioning parts of his family, but the cancerous artifacts of his lost daughter. And it's crippling his home life. Look at what it did to Margaret. When she finally tried to pack up some of Tamara's belongings, Paul's remorse quickly curdled. The pain of letting these material memories go was too much for him, blinding him to the love of his own wife—nearly blinding *her* in return.

Doesn't take long for our misery to mold. Does it, Paul? It rankles into anger within the snap of a finger. *(Snap.)* Missing Tamara for all these years has given your grief a target, something your sorrow can always aim for—while knowing quite well that, wherever she is, your daughter is not coming back.

Your children won't be coming home, folks. They won't be waiting for you at your doorstep when you roll into the driveway tonight, you're not going to find them huddled in the headlights when they flash past the front porch. You will be returning to an empty nest for the rest of your lives.

Now, if we could just sever that hope from our hearts once and for all, then we will have made the first move toward walking off this *path of pain*. It's not a step, mind you. The revelation of losing a loved one is really the step-*before*-the-step. It *initiates* the turnaround. Once we recognize the fact that our children will never set foot into our houses again, *then* we can finally begin our own healing.

So what do we think that first step could be, gang?

Hmm? Paul's pretty warm. Margaret felt it, firsthand.

Come on, guys. We don't need to raise our hands, here. Just because we meet in an elementary school doesn't mean we have to act like we're in the fifth grade. Don't make me call on one of you like I was your teacher. We made this decision to mend ourselves. *Why* are we here? Because we want to stop hurting. And *how* do we stop hurting? We face this situation, head-on. Because we've been avoiding ourselves enough, as is. Don't you think? It takes a certain courage to look inward, to see ourselves for what we've become because of our ordeals. *That* is the first step. If we can face ourselves, then I believe we're finally ready to move forward. And to do that, we need strength. And *where* do we find our strength?

Guys?

We find it inside. We search through ourselves until we discover the one thing that *compels* us to keep living. Something in your heart is giving you the strength to be here tonight. It could be a promise you made to your wife. Even a photo of your family that you keep in your wallet. For me, it's my daughter Angela. I know I've mentioned her to the group before. She's ten now. Finally reached the double digits last month. She gives me the strength to guide our group off this *path of pain*. To lead each and every one of you back on track to your own lives. And I thank God for every day that I have her in my life.

So think of the one thing that gives *you* the courage to be here. Go ahead. Visualize it, right now.

Got it? Good.

Now close your eyes. Just for a second. I want you to hear something.

Before you come in every night, I pull these chairs out and unfold them—the creak in the hinges ringing through this empty auditorium. I get this image in my head that I'm gathering up a bunch of twigs and branches, building a nest for the rest of us. A place where we can feel safe. We form a ring for a reason, folks. This is our *circle of strength*. When we sit inside it, we don't ever have to worry over hurting alone. We're linked. Our losses have become a ligament to one another, these incidents that have brought us here, binding us together. We let go of our grief through sharing our stories, feeding our confessions to each other like they were worms dangling from a mother bird's beak. No matter how different our ordeals may be from one another's, we devour them all—swallowing every detail as if we survived off of them, as if we were dependent on them. Like food.

We go home with a belly full of each other's remorse. We bring that grief back into our own houses. And we digest it. We nourish ourselves on knowing we're not alone. That, with Tamara or Josh or Spence gone—we have each other now. We have our group.

And it's feeding time every Wednesday.

Want to know what's the hardest part about these meetings? For me, it's listening to these chairs. They're so old. The wood groans whenever one of us shifts in their seat. They've probably been in this school since it first opened, decades ago. Before any of your kids were students here, I bet. Years before. Who knows. Maybe one of us is sitting in the same seat they used once. Maybe, if we sifted through every single chair, we might find their names scratched into the wood. Maybe Tamara scribbled the name of her first crush on the back paneling. Did you ever think of that, Margaret? You never know.

But listen to the way the wood bends beneath us. They're squealing, almost. These seats weren't built for so much weight, were they? These are children's chairs. Think about how they must sound when a six-year-old sits in them. They probably don't make a peep. But when we squeeze in, it's as if we are hurting them. When it comes time to fold up the chairs at the end of the night, I always hesitate right before I reach for that first seat, asking myself, *what's going to happen to all that grief we released tonight, when I break our circle of strength? Where will all that remorse go if I rip open this ring?* It feels unfair to me that we're here in this school, saying the things we do in these chairs, when tomorrow, some kid is going to sit down in the same seat Paul did. My own daughter could be in this very chair tomorrow morning. And what's to stop her from soaking up some of his sorrow? What's going to keep Angela from feeling it herself?

She's getting to that inquisitive point where she has to ask a question about everything—like, *Why's the sky blue?* or *What does daddy do for a living?*

You know what? I've never told her. About what I do. About any of you. What am I supposed to say? Should I share Tamara? How she hopped into some boy's van and never came home? Should I explain what it's put her parents through for the last five years? How they have to bury her in their hearts and realize that she's dead, just so they can get on with their own lives? Or there's always Josh. His story's simple enough. During a game of hide-and-go-seek, he slipped inside his neighbor's old refrigerator, rusting in his backyard. Eight hours after the game had been called off and everyone on the block was beginning to get tired of searching, someone finally decided to check the fridge. Josh toppled out, the smell of his own feces following along. He shat in his pants, he'd been so scared in there. Now every time his parents reach for the door to their own fridge, they're afraid they're going to find him inside, huddled on the rack, waiting for them.

What could I possibly tell Angela that would make her understand what happens here? I realized it'd be easier for her to believe I was a veterinarian instead—telling her that I help heal injured animals rather than explain that I sit here, in her own school, listening to all of you.

Because *look* at you. This group's become a feeding frenzy for fragmented families. You're all pecking at each other's pasts as if you were plucking the worms out from the ground above your own children's graves, feeding off these feelings like they were the only meal you could stomach. If you can't keep your kids at home, you'll keep them around by coming here. You dangle the memories of your own child to the rest of us—and we snap at the chance to chew through, just waiting for our turn to toss out our own little mournful morsel.

So Paul. What do *you* have to share with the group tonight? You've always got an earful for the rest of us. Five years is enough time for every possible explanation to infest itself inside your imagination, breeding more and more reasons why Tamara might've run away. The possibilities have probably propagated among themselves, squirming under your skull. Like maggots. They fed on your hope through all these years. Whatever little kernel you were keeping in your heart, what simple sliver of a silent prayer you save for those days when you drive to work or when you're in the shower—your sorrow only chews through it, your grief eating your hope for its own sustenance. And look at what it's done to you and Margaret. You're so worm-ridden with remorse, your bodies have hollowed out into husks of human beings.

Who did we agree was the corpse, here? Who did we decide had died, so the two of you could start living again?

You don't want to heal. None of you do. You'd rather keep grieving. It's the only way any of you can feel like you're alive anymore.

Well, I have a life beyond these meetings. I still have a family. My daughter's at home, sleeping as we speak—tucked in so tightly, her sheets might as well be strapping her down to the bed. The moment I pull into my driveway, I have to rush right up to her room, just to make sure she's still there. I'll stand at her door for hours, simply watching her sleep—thanking God for keeping her at home. After leading this group for years, I think I've finally taken home my fill of misery. I won't allow your sorrow into my house or anywhere near her ears. Nothing out here feels safe to me anymore. Not even her own elementary school. If I have to holster my daughter into her bed until she turns twenty, then fine. I'll feed her every meal from my own mouth, if I have to—dangling dinner down to her from between my teeth. I'm willing to take that step before Angela ends up like your children. And I end up like you.

I'm tired of feeding you hope. Because look at what you've become. You're all scrambling over top of each other, wrestling for that last crumb of consanguinity from your kids' corpses. Anything to keep you weeping. But once this group runs out of remorse, there won't be anyone else for us to turn to. So we'll turn on ourselves. And we'll peck and peck and peck at each other until we find that familiar pang of parenthood all over again—

yanking up that nerve until we remember what it was like when there was someone to hurt over. We'll pluck at our past until we tap into that pain that reminds us we're still alive. And we'll all call it progress. *Healing*.

So. Who wants to share first?

georgia

So come on down to Daddy Rabbit's tonight, where the beer is on tap and the women are always ready to please. Partake in some of Georgia's finest peaches, the one and only Daddy Rabbit's all-nude review—seven days a week, from morning till night. Tell the bartender you heard our ad on the radio and receive your second drink for half off. Every Wednesday night is Ladies Night here at Daddy Rabbit's, where you gals can come in for free. Wet T-shirt contest every night, starting at eleven. Contestants can sign up at the door to waive the price of admission. It doesn't get any better than this, boys—so what are you waiting for? Hop on down to Daddy Rabbit's today!

philip winters

My memories would be better served if they were like radio stations. With just a turn of the dial, I could tune in to them all over again. One Christmas, I'd bought Delila a new toaster. Better than the one we already had. Can't really remember what was wrong with our old one, other than the lid would always unhinge, so the crust closest to the outside wouldn't be as toasted as the rest of the bread. I never throw away anything—especially if it's not really broken—so I ended up stashing the old toaster in the basement, while Delila plugged the new one in.

A couple of months later, Edey accidentally knocked it to the ground. Lucky for us I had kept the old one. We'd have half-toasted toast for breakfast for as long as it took us to buy a new one, which was better than having no toast at all. I found it in the basement, buried under a month's worth of junk. Plugged it right back in and we were golden brown all over again.

The next morning, at breakfast, I remember the four of us all sitting at the table. There was a rough smell in the air, like something burning. It was obviously coming from the toaster. I figured it was just dust settling over the heating coils, which would eventually burn off. I told everyone not to worry about it.

But you were the first of us to bite into their toast. In the middle of chewing, this funny look spread over your face. You spit out your mouthful. A lump of bread and jam rolled across the table as you reached for your orange juice, gulping down half of the glass before you even took a breath. Nearly choking, you started spitting out whatever was left in your mouth.

"My toast tastes like burned hot dogs," you said in between spits.

Delila wasn't quick enough to stop Edey from biting into her own slice. Jelly and soggy bread sputtered out of Edey's mouth in a half-spit, toppling down her chin. She started crying, her open mouth lined in chunks of spit-soaked bread.

I picked up my own piece of toast. Bringing it to my nose, I sniffed. It smelled like charred flesh.

Opening the toaster, the scent wafted out—acrid, like a barbecue gone wrong. Underneath the heating coils was the charred carcass of a mouse, all curled up and black. There was barely any skin left to the bone, shrink-wrapped in its own flesh. It must've crawled in through the loose door, trapping itself inside and starving to death—only to end up getting cremated for breakfast.

You'd gotten your first taste of death, Kevin. The actual flavor of it was on your tongue, fuzzy and numbing.

Delila always used to say I was being overprotective, prophesizing that you would resent me for it when you got older. I'd ask her what she thought I should do when it came to raising you, what she would do differently. *How do you raise a sickly kid?* It wasn't as if I was keeping you from your friends. Invitations to sleepovers were in short supply for you all throughout elementary school. When you were in the fifth grade, Joshua Raymond asked you over to his house for a slumber party, along with all the other boys from your T-ball team. It was a first for you. You could barely hold your asthma back, you were so excited. Simply thinking about spending the night at Josh's house thinned your breath down to shallow pants, the weight of an all-nighter bearing down on your chest. Mom packed you an extra inhaler, just in case, while I got to drive you over. The Raymonds' house wasn't so far away from ours. Most kids could've walked there. But I wanted to drop you off, make sure that you got to their front door safely.

On the way I said, "Remember to thank Mrs. Raymond for letting you stay over."

"Okay."

I went around the block an extra time, acting as if I'd accidentally passed their house.

"Dad! You just missed it."

"You know not to sneak out when Josh's parents go to bed. I don't care if everyone else does—you stay inside tonight. No horseplaying at two in the morning."

"Okay."

"Don't forget to brush your teeth."

"*Okay*, Dad . . ."

This would be your first night out from under our roof, sleeping at someone else's house without us. "I think I'll come up and say hello to Wendy."

"Can't you say hello to her when you pick me up tomorrow?"

"I just want to make sure she knows about your asthma."

"Dad, everybody knows about my asthma . . ."

On the drive home, I started to remember all the pranks I pulled when I spent the night over at a friend's house. Toilet papering people's front lawns, squirting shaving cream across neighbors' windows. When I was your age, these slumber parties were simply excuses to slip outside in the middle of the night, running down the streets well after everyone else in our neighborhood had fallen asleep. I imagined you doing the same. I wondered what would happen if you got caught ringing someone's doorbell, how you would react if you were chased down the street—if your lungs would hold up long enough to make it back to Josh's house. Your inhaler would be waiting for you there, tucked inside a plastic baggy along with your toothbrush. I saw you scrambling over lawns, slipping on wet grass, muddying up your knees. The rest of your friends would be houses ahead of you, racing back to safety, as you trailed behind more and more, stumbling over your own lungs. You'd be the first to get caught, the runt of the litter. I went to bed worrying over your chances of surviving your first sleepover, envisioning those kids squirting toothpaste down your underwear after you fell asleep or pouring warm water in your hand in hopes of you wetting yourself.

When the phone rang an hour later, I expected it to be the paramedics calling us to come down to the hospital.

"Dad . . ."

"Is everything okay, Kevin?"

"Can you come pick me up? I want to come home."

When I knocked on the Raymonds' door, Wendy greeted me almost immediately. "Hello, Phil. Sorry for making you come out so late."

"No worries, Wendy. Hope we didn't keep you up."

"No, no—it's fine. Kevin was just getting a little homesick, that's all. I would've driven him home myself, but he insisted he call you."

You slipped past Wendy without saying goodbye, your sleeping bag bundled up in your arms.

The ride home was quiet. You stared out your window, the occasional sniffle lifting up from your nose. I didn't ask any questions, deciding to drive to the local mini-mart and pick up a pint of rocky road ice cream for us to share. With a plastic spoon between us, we ate the whole thing right there in the parking lot. Eventually, the sniffles dissipated, the redness in your cheeks sinking back into their pale complexion. You even smiled once. The clock on the dashboard said it was eleven-thirty, which was well past both of our bedtimes. You fell asleep about five blocks away from our house—your eyes struggling to stay open, only to forfeit just before pulling into the driveway. Turning the engine off, I sat back and watched you sleep—curled up into your seat, your sleeping bag pillowing your head. You looked so peaceful just then, I didn't want to wake you. I suddenly felt ashamed for wanting you to come home as badly as I had, as if it'd been my fault for turning you around. The sound of your voice over the telephone had a sense of dejection inside it, like you had given up on braving the outside world—ready to sulk back to the safety of your own home. The more I thought about what you'd said to me, the way the receiver made it seem as if you were ashamed to ask—*Can you come pick me up? I want to come home*—as if home was the last place you wanted to be.

Unleashing you from your seat belt was difficult, your arms woven within the shoulder strap. The moment I unbuckled you, your body toppled forward. I caught you, carrying you back inside our house, your head buried in my neck. Tucking you into bed, I kept the door to your room open, allowing the hallway light to slip inside that crack, just in case you woke up wondering where I was.

Ever played One-Eyed Willie before? My family would have at this game every time we took a road trip together. It's easy. Look for a car with one of its headlights out. If you see one, touch the roof of the car and say *One-Eyed Willie!* Each one you get scores you a point. Whoever gets the most points wins. Simple enough, right?

Let's play.

One-Eyed Willie!

One-Eyed Willie.

Come on, Kevin. You're not even trying. There are dozens of cars with only one headlight out here on the highway. We've passed at least five of them within the last ten minutes. They're staring you down from the oncoming traffic. With their one burned-out bulb, they look just like your own eyeball sunk into the socket—probably playing the same game with you.

the mourning glory group: I on you

Hello. My name is Paul Clark. This is my wife, Margaret. We were Tamara's parents.

Putting her in the past tense has been tough. The only place we haven't been able to bury our daughter has been within our mouths. It doesn't sound right rolling off my tongue, just yet—admitting that she's dead, hearing myself say it out loud. But we're working on it. We're trying.

Tamara was going out on her first date with Kevin Winters when they had their accident. The two of them and a few friends all piled into Kevin's car, putting that asthmatic behind the wheel. I'm positive my daughter wouldn't have gotten into the van if that boy had been drinking, so I know there wasn't any alcohol involved. I'd taught Tamara to know better than that. She was a smart girl.

All us parents keep looking for an explanation over how this could've happened—while I know for a fact that Kevin had been having one of his asthma attacks that night. He must've been suffocating himself when he ran his van right through the guardrail next to the road, sending them all toppling into the swamp. I blame his breathing problems for all this. If it wasn't for his lungs, I wouldn't be sitting here with the rest of my neighborhood now—talking ourselves in circles. I'd be at home with my daughter. My family would be intact.

You should've heard him wheeze. When Kevin came to pick Tamara up that night, he must've been nervous. The air just wouldn't go down his throat. He had to use his inhaler before he shook my hand, his breath smelling metallic when he greeted me. I'd been sniffing for alcohol, not Albuterol. Kissing him would be like licking nickels. I couldn't understand what Tamara saw in the boy, especially with as limp of a wrist as he had. I didn't even realize I was shaking his clammy hand, until his sweat rubbed off in my palm. *When you're giving a firm handshake, look the man straight in the eye*. That's what my dad told me. Kevin couldn't even lift his chin up from his chest. His eyes never went above my collarbone.

And I'm supposed to feel confident about letting this boy escort my daughter out of my house? Meeting the family. The night I was first introduced to my wife's father, I remember packing an extra pair of boxer shorts in the glove compartment of my car. That way, once we got to the movies, I could slip into the restroom and switch the fresh pair for the ones I'd soiled. No lie. I'd heard stories about Margaret's dad well before asking her out. The boys at my high school had built up legends around the man. They said to me, if I left the Archibald house without shitting in my pants, I was a lucky, *lucky* man.

Margaret's father wanted to arm wrestle me before I even took her out on our first date. I've known this man for about ten minutes, not a second more. And he's threatening me. We were alone in the living room, while Margaret and her mother were in the kitchen, and he flat-out challenges me to a match. He swipes the magazines off the coffee table and plants his elbow down, right in front of me.

That was as much of a warning as I got. I *had* to follow through.

It all came down to respect. It did then, and it most definitely still does now. Should I let the man win and think his daughter's dating a sap? Or do I bowl him over and never get the chance to see his girl again? If I threw in the towel before even stepping into the ring, old Archibald would never look me in the eye again. And I knew he could sniff out a fixed fight. You could just tell from looking at him.

But if I took his hand down to the table, cracking his knuckles over top his own furniture—that he worked hard to pay for—he'd think twice about allowing his daughter to get in the car with me.

So what was I going to be? A tapeworm or a roughnecker?

No matter how frightened of him I was at that very moment, I respected the man. For putting me in a situation like that, let me tell you, it was clear that he loved his daughter. Not only did I have to think quick, but I had to think *right*. When it came down to me and old Archibald, I let him win. Sure, I broke some sweat and gave him a few scares—but I let him win at arm wrestling, so I could win over his daughter. And it laid down the foundation for my family.

So when little Kevin Winters walked into my home, the man that would end up running her off the road, I wanted him to *earn* my respect. I wanted to see if he *deserved* my daughter.

Tamara hadn't been ready, which left the two of us some time to talk. He wasn't going to say anything unless I said it first, so I just came out with it, *"I am a little nervous about taking your daughter out tonight, sir."*

He looked confused, like I'd read his mind. It was written all over his face, for Christ's sake. Wasn't so hard. The sweat on his forehead was a fucking billboard for his nervousness.

"Go ahead and say it," I told him. "Might as well break the tension in here before we start suffocating. Don't you think?" His cheeks had been blue up until Tamara left the room. I wanted my daughter to go out on this date, I did. What I *wasn't* looking for was this boy passing out on her. At least it gave us some time to get to know each other, right? Man to man? These introductions are so awkward to begin with. First impressions used to always kill me when I was a kid.

"So humor me," I said. "*I'm a little nervous about taking your daughter out tonight, sir.*" I just wanted to hear him say it. It would've made me feel more comfortable to hear the words come out from his mouth. I was about to leave my only daughter in his hands, here—so I just wanted to see how shaky those hands really were.

"Don't worry. Just loosen up a little. Tamara's nervous, too. Believe me. She wants this night to be special. She's brought you into our home, Kevin. Now that's a big step. She's brought you here to me. She's crazy about you—you know that? For weeks now, she's been coming home from school, hardly able to think about anything else. When it comes time for her to bring home her report card, you better make sure you're grading her on something. Because at this point the only class she's likely to pass is Kevin 101."

She'd never had a boyfriend before. Not as serious as this. Not serious enough to bring home to me. You had to understand how insecure she was about all of this—and I didn't blame her. Tamara was not beautiful in a very conventional way. She didn't have the looks that people are passing off as pretty nowadays. It would take some time to get to know her before you could see how wonderful a girl she really was—and not many people were willing to make that effort. Beauty that isn't skin deep is going to be overlooked by most kids in high school. But Tamara told me Kevin was different. He had supposedly seen this special side of her, which must've made him pretty important. She didn't open up to that many people. Especially not to boys.

"Why do you think that is, Kevin?" I asked him. "Why doesn't my daughter open up to more boys? What I wouldn't give to be in your shoes right now! Up until Tamara met you, she'd come home from school crying. She'd have nightmares about getting on the bus the next morning.

"Why do boys make fun of her?

"What's so awkward about my little girl?"

His eyes began to wander around the room, looking for something to save him from our conversation. "Has she told you about her lazy eye yet? You've at least noticed it, right? When you're talking to her, does her right eye ever wander away from you? I'll fill you in on a little secret, okay? Just between you and me. When she was younger, Tamara had accidentally slipped in the bathtub. I'd been the one washing her. I made her stand up so I could give her a good scrub and she just slipped through my hands. Fell right back into the tub, hitting her head on the faucet. Cracked her vision in half for good. When I picked her up, I held her in my hands—my right cradling her fractured cranium, my left holding the rest of her. I ran right out into the street, stopping the first car that drove by, insisting that they take us to the hospital. Her eyesight's been split ever since. Most people now don't even notice it. Or won't. They'll think she's not paying attention to them, looking the other away. But that's not true at all. She listens to everything. She listens to me better than anyone I've ever met. Whenever we're having a conversation with each other, I never feel like I'm talking to a little girl. She's always been an adult to me. So the next time you and Tamara have a chat (maybe tonight, after the movie, in your car, when you bring her home, while you two are saying goodbye, and you feel like giving her a kiss), I want you to think of this: You and me—we're sharing now. She's going to look at you with every feeling she's never been able to understand until now. Every burst of warmth that comes with the mere sight of you, those dainty hands, those pale cheeks—she'll give you all that back within a simple blink.

"But the lazy eye is for me. Okay? It's Daddy's little stray coming home. And you'll never be able to stop her. You got that? We can split. I'm fine with that. But she's mine before she's yours."

I wanted him to understand what I was saying. "Before the two of you leave, I bet you're going to need to use our bathroom. When you do, pay attention to the tub on your right. Try to imagine what happened there, eleven years ago. Just picture her as a little girl—standing there, wearing nothing but the suds from my sponge as I wiped her body down. I want you to try and imagine what it must've felt like to have her slip right through my hands, losing my grip. If you can even fathom the sound her head made when she hit the porcelain, her skull cracking across the spigot, then you and me can talk about who's earned her love.

"There's going to come a day when she's going to share everything I've just told you, all on her own. When she tells you about how it all happened—you're going to be such an understanding boyfriend, aren't you? You'll listen to her. It'll be as if you knew exactly what she was going to say before she even says it. You'll be that good of a guy, won't you, Kevin?

"Better not let me down, Kevin. I'm only trying to help you here. I'm just giving you a couple of pointers, that's all. Take it or leave it. This is my daughter we're talking about, here. I want you to treat her right."

His face had turned blue. His lips lost all their blood. He

brought his inhaler up to his mouth and got a good puff of the stuff. He was frightened of me, I could tell. I'd made him think twice about laying a hand on my daughter, which was all I was after. I figured Tamara would've been ready by then, so when she hadn't come downstairs yet, I just kept improvising. Half of what I said simply popped up into my head, right there on the spot. Bullshit never sounded sweeter.

Tamara finally came down, all dressed up. They were just going to a movie. She didn't need to put on that much makeup, especially if she was going to be sitting in the dark the whole time. But staring at Tamara just then, she looked exactly like her mother when we'd gone out on our first date. She looked beautiful. My little girl was all grown up.

If I really want to hurt myself over letting her go out that night, I think of her underwater. With all that makeup painted on her face, I wonder what she must've looked like as time went by and she began to bloat. I wonder if her cheeks kept pink or if her eyeliner ran. I think about how red her lips must've been through everything, considering that Margaret let her borrow her makeup, a brand that doesn't smudge—even when you're drinking. With all of that water rushing down her throat, my daughter must've put that lipstick to the test. Five years later and her lips are still ready for Kevin to kiss her goodnight.

philip winters

Started having car trouble a few miles across the Georgia state line. Heard the engine begin to hack up oil just outside of Jessup, coughing out the old phlegm collecting deep within its chest. The transmission would wheeze whenever its speed extended beyond fifty miles an hour. We'd been traveling nonstop since this morning, my foot fastened to the gas pedal, climbing up I-95 for almost twelve hours straight. No bathroom breaks, no breakfast. Just driving—you, me, and the automobile reaching up for South Carolina.

Putting my hand on the dashboard, I could feel how warm the car was. It was overheating more and more with every mile. I wanted to say, *Tell me if I'm pushing you too hard. It's no problem to pull over*. It refused to give up, determined to drive. Letting me down was worse than breaking down. There was that constant hum from underneath the hood, the motor hitting this high pitch that sounded so much like an asthma attack, its chest resonating with the rattle of phlegmy metal—the engine straining to keep itself from suffocating.

I'd become familiar with that sound. I couldn't help hearing it wherever I went. The line dividing the two of you began to blur for me, the differences between my boy and my automobile slipping, until you were practically the same. The two of you could've been brothers.

When you were younger and we were driving somewhere, we'd always sing this song. "The ankle bone is connected to the *foot* bone, the foot bone is connected to the *gas pedal* bone, the gas pedal bone is connected to the *transmission* bone, the transmission bone is connected to the *engine* bone, the engine bone is connected to the *steering axle* bone, the steering axle bone is connected to the *steering wheel* bone, the steering wheel bone is connected to the *hand* bone, the hand bone is connected to the *wrist* bone, the wrist bone is connected to the *arm* bone, the arm bone is connected to the *shoulder* bone, the shoulder bone is connected to the *back* bone, the back bone is connected to the . . . *butt* bone, the butt bone is connected to the *leg* bone, the leg bone is connected to the *ankle* bone . . ."

It dawned on me that I hadn't changed the oil in a while. What transmission fluid was still flowing through would dry up, dehydrating the car. The wheezing was worsening, the rattle from the engine vibrating through the rest of the car.

We were coming up to a Texaco on the right. Its sign hung over the highway, its colors all faded from years' worth of weather—looking like some scarecrow standing above a field full of broken-down cars. Rows of old automobiles stretched out behind the gas station, filling up this field as far as I could see. Cars were piled on top of one another, sometimes three or four high. Their paint chipped off like skin flaking away from the bone. Broken glass had scattered over the ground, like loose teeth lost in the grass. The sunlight caught each one, while the jaws of so many shattered windows were left barren, broken. Just gums. Windshield wipers were jutting out like eyelashes left attached at the empty sockets of so many hollowed chassis.

Never had the nerve to say a prayer for a car before, but looking into this scrap heap made me think differently. Nobody cared about these cars. These are the runaways, the strays. I pictured their parents at home, the owners of all these automobiles waiting by the window for years, wondering where their children were. I had to stop and thank God that you hadn't ended up in one of these junkyards, Kevin.

I parked in front of the pumps, stepping out for the first time since I'd gotten into the car earlier that morning. You never realize how sore you are until you get to stretch. There was an ache within me, all over. This heat wasn't helping. Georgia humidity. It was leaving my skin stickier than flypaper. Even with the engine turned off, I could still hear the car catching its breath—the air thick inside its chest, hooked and unable to flow freely. One of the worst asthma attacks I'd ever heard.

Looking around, I couldn't find someone to help. There was nobody around. I didn't know if the station was even open anymore. Weeds were working their way out from the cracks in the asphalt, growing over the parking lot to the point of overtaking the pavement. I couldn't find a car that looked like it could run, every automobile in sight either gutted or stripped. No license plates, no state tags. There was a pile of tires stacked against the side of the station. Most of the cars out back were lying on their axles, limbless.

Then came the first caw. It lifted up from one of the cars, slightly vibrating through the metal. Then another, off to the left. Now I could hear the sound of scraping steel. I could suddenly see a scattered number of crows hopping out from inside the cavities of those cars, perching themselves where they could see this fresh piece of machinery, eyeing my automobile as if it were about to die. The fast breathing of my baby was a lullaby to those birds, that death rattle from the engine ringing like a dinner bell. They'd be swooping down before too much longer, clawing onto the upholstery and ripping off what they could grab—ripping my car apart. This was just as good as some piece of roadkill left rotting by the side of the highway. A car would take decades to deteriorate. The meat clinging to its metal would keep for years. These crows could roost within its ribs, building a nest in its belly—and never have to worry over it ever crawling away.

"You've been piling some miles onto this baby, haven't you?" An old man walked out from inside the station, his shoulders hunched over.

"Do you sell motor oil here?" I asked.

"Sell it? I'd give it away, if that's all it took for some company."

I bought two quarts. I poured the fluid in through a paper funnel I picked up from the ground, spilling a drip over the engine. For a moment, I was reminded of the times when I'd watch Delila breast-feed you, Kevin—sipping straight from the nipple, your lips locked onto her body, that little bit of milk dribbling down your cheek.

"Looks like your car could use a good once-over before you hit the road again. There's definitely a leak, but that's easy to fix. I'm sure I could take a walk out back and pull up the right piece. Wouldn't take more than a minute."

My stomach turned. *Walk out back and pull up the right piece.* This man was just like some grave robber, sifting through those old cars as if he was harvesting parts.

"I've tried putting together a car of my own with my spare time. I'm sitting on enough parts to build me a caravan, all for my own." He wiped his hands with a greasy rag. The oil was so deep in its tint, the color kept to his skin, staining his wrinkles a dark purple. There was oil puddling up on the pavement. When the sun struck the liquid, the colors that swirled up from inside were hypnotizing. Out of that black, I saw pinks, greens, purples—fluctuating the longer I looked at it. The pigment would change, depending on where I stood. I imagined this man to be some backwoods mad scientist, this off-road Frankenstein that the rest of the world had forgotten. These cars were the closest he could come to companionship. It stung to hear him call these cars *she*. It was in the way he said it, somehow. As if he had never touched a real woman before. He seemed to lean in with the word—his jaw jutting just enough to stretch the sound out a little more than he should. He was building his own plaything back here. His own blow-up doll. The junkyard out back was nothing more than a body shop for this one perfect machine.

"How much do I owe you?"

There was a moment when he almost looked hurt, as if he took my eagerness to get back on the road personally. "How 'bout you just give me ten and we call it even?"

I spy something gray.

The asphalt, right. All that tar.

Okay. Now, I spy something . . . green.

The grass. You got it.

I spy something . . . brown.

On the right. Out the window.

The mud in the ditches. Yep.

Okay, okay . . . Here's one. I spy something white. White. Look low. Lower. They're right under us.

The divider lines. There you go. Good going, Kevin.

Now your turn.

I spy something gray . . .

Your bones. You soaked up so much water, it left your flesh pretty flimsy. It couldn't hold your body together anymore. Your bones had begun to split through your skin—poking out at your shoulders, your knees. They became discolored from the exposure to the air. They didn't look so white anymore. Just waterlogged. So sodden and rotten, they've gone gray. Black around the more moist spots. Like those big bruises you got on your knees when you were younger. Delila and I had decided to get you your first bike for your fifth birthday, surprising you with it when you got back home from school. You were itching to ride it like all the big kids around you, without the training wheels—nearly pitching a fit when I put them on. You begged me to take them off, crying, swearing that you were old enough to ride without them. So I went ahead and let you. I would hold the back of your seat while you pedaled, running along behind you, trying to keep you balanced as much as I could without hindering the ride. I was your training wheel, whether you knew it or not. You were laughing so much, exhilarated from the speeds you were reaching, that when I accidentally let go and you kept going, faster and faster, you thought it was all a part of the trip. Then the sidewalk dipped, pulling the front tire down enough for your body to lean over the handlebars. You tumbled to the asphalt. You scraped your elbow, cut your chin. Both of your knees bruised up so much, turning purple and black and gray, you refused to wear shorts for weeks. We put the training wheels back on the bike, but you rarely ever rode it after that.

I spy something green.

The algae on your face. This moss must've started growing over your body underwater, reaching into the deeper crevices, spreading outward. The joints around your jawbone. Just a slight film, here and there. Nothing too thick. Nothing a little scrubbing won't get rid of. We'll scrape it away when the time comes. It's just like cleaning the potatoes out from your ears, that's all. When I had to wash you in the tub, I'd take a hand towel and scrub back behind your ears—reaching around for all of those hard-to-clean spots. I'd never leave an inch of your skin unturned in the tub, washing everything. You even made a song up about it. We'd sing it together, while I cleaned your ears—"Scrubbing the dirt behind my (your) ears, behind my (your) ears, behind my (your) ears. Scrubbing the dirt behind my (your) ears, I'm (you're) a clee-ean bo-oy." When I'd wash your hair, we'd sing the same—"Washing the dirt out of my (your) hair, out of my (your) hair, out of my (your) hair. Washing the dirt out of my (your) hair, I'm (you're) a clee-ean bo-oy."

Washing the moss from your jaw, from your jaw, from your jaw. Washing the moss from your jaw, you're a clee-ean bo-oy.

I spy something brown.

The mud seeping out through your teeth. Your skull's a pocket for swamp water right now. The sludge keeps spilling out over the seat. You're pretty much sitting in a puddle of muck. Can't help but think back to that one time you and Spence Partridge spent the day making mud pies in our backyard. You were both covered in dirt by dinnertime. It had rubbed into your hair, all over your clothes. You guys had stacked the pies high, though. I bet you made over a dozen each. Leaving them out in the sun had got them to harden, like you'd baked them in the oven. After you guys washed up, you went back outside only to find your pies all brittle and brown. You and Spence set up a stand by the side of the road and tried selling them to people who'd drive by, a quarter a pie. Whenever someone would actually pull over, they'd think you were pushing brownies or cookies. Not earth. Not dirt.

So no one was buying. After seeing the disappointed look on both of your faces, I decided to purchase them all. I gave you guys two dollars each for the whole stack. Once you were in bed for the night, I took the chunks of clay out into the backyard, dumping them into the mud. The morass swallowed the pies up, hungry for them—soaking through the dry dirt, turning them into mush all over again. Digesting them. I don't think I ever admitted it to you. Probably, I felt as if you'd be mad at me for not keeping them. You asked me the next day what I had done with your pies, and I think I told you I'd eaten them all. Your eyes widened, looking at me with this admiration—as if you were proud that I had, for believing in you.

I spy something white.

Your skin. All that loose wrapping, splitting open. What's left of your flesh is as white as a blister, white all over. It reminds me of when we took off your first Band-Aid. Can't really remember what you had cut yourself on. A kitchen knife, I think. But you had that Band-Aid on your finger for a week, refusing to remove it. You'd been wearing it for so long, all these loose hairs were clinging to the sticky edges, some grit lining the ends. When we decided it was high time to peel it off, you wanted to make a ceremony out of it—the magic of healing happening right underneath the bandage. The cut would've vanished in a big disappearing act, *poof*. The color of your fingertip was so pale in comparison to the rest of your hand, the skin looked like it hadn't seen the sun in years. All white and wrinkled. The Band-Aid had been on so tight, it cinched off the flow of blood from your finger.

I always wondered about your lungs, son. How tender they were to me. We never knew what to shield you from, how best we could protect your breath. We didn't know if it was safe to take you outside during the summer, sucking in all that pollen—or if it was smart to keep you inside with all the dust swirling through the air. Your asthma was a mystery to me.

You hated your inhalers—I remember that. At first, you refused to use them at all, swearing they embarrassed you, because none of your other friends ever needed them. An attack would come on—your throat cinching up, your lungs shriveling—and you would just shake your head away from your mother's hand as she held out your inhaler. You'd pinch your lips and close your eyes, your skin turning blue the longer you insisted on staying away from your medication. There were times when we'd have to take you to the doctor, just because you wouldn't use them at all—preferring to pass out rather than sip some of that battery acid.

Then we took you to the beach one day. The whole family was spread out along the shore—you, me, Mom, and Edey, all sitting on our own towels, catching some sun. This pack of scuba divers caught your eye. You saw the tanks strapped to their backs, the mouthpiece funneling the oxygen to their lungs. Turning to me, you slipped your inhaler in between your lips—holding it there so that the canister pointed toward your ear. With eyes so wide, you jumped up from your towel and ran right for the ocean, diving into the water with your own air tank.

We all watched you swim out, then dipping your head below. You'd been down there for a while. Your body hadn't broken over the surface—your foot or your hand hadn't poked through. No second breath since you first went under.

The idea popped into my mind, raising my temperature. It wasn't even a question. It was a notion, concrete—I knew you were drowning. I was suddenly so certain of it. Standing up, I went right for the water. Once I was up to my waist, I dove in with the deepest breath my lungs could hold. It was murky down there. A cloud of sand spiraled through a beam of sun, like dust caught in the light coming through the window.

When Delila found you walking along the beach, discovering that the tide had just dragged you down-shore—your inhaler still in your mouth, I think I'd finally accepted the fact that your lungs weren't built to breathe. They never had been. The water was a better home for you than the land.

I've been picturing you at the bottom of the swamp, settling in the mud. You could've kept yourself alive by simply using your inhaler. While the lungs of all the other children filled up with muck, yours were preserved, airtight—thanks to your asthma. They reminded me of formaldehyde. If your prescription hadn't run out, those inhalers could've been the best embalming fluid around.

south carolina

Traffic for the hour is a bit cluttered around Highway 52 and Interstate 95. Our eye-in-the-sky Fred Tanner recommends keeping clear of the intersection for at least until three this afternoon. Rush hour is only going to makes matters worse for those poor road construction folks, trying valiantly to make our highways a better place to spend your commute . . . This next song goes out to the fellas in Kingstree, toiling under that hot South Carolina sun. We'll start the hour off with a block of songs requested by all you people out there. Feel free to give us a ring and add your favorite tune to the list. We'll be taking calls all day long, right here on . . .

the mourning glory group: ward and wendy raymond

My wife and I have been coming to these meetings for a few years now. Gotten familiar with everyone's face here, pretty much. I've even come to consider a couple of you people as my good friends. I know Wendy has. Folks you don't mind inviting over to your home—throw a barbecue for the whole neighborhood when the weather's warm enough. People like Paul and Margaret. Tom and Stacy. *Good* people.

But, then again . . . some of us go back before this group even started. I'm talking about T-ball. The Delray Devils. District all-stars, three years in a row. Back when I was coach, I took our kids all the way to the state finals. Won twice, too. Had our uniforms made up with the money from my own pocket, because let me tell you—when my son was out there in that field, his head held up high, looking out for that pop fly to fall right into his mitt, his lungs gripping his breath until he caught the ball—*those* were the priceless moments when coaching your kids was worth every penny. Just to see Josh play. He told me once he was embarrassed that he even needed the T—itching for a real pitch so much, he asked me if I'd toss him the ball instead. Just so he wouldn't have to pretend anymore. My son was yearning to go pro by age nine. He brought home enough trophies to fill up our living room. I had to build an extra shelf for each new season, just to keep up with him. You should see them all lined up alongside each other, a whole row running the length of our wall. Twenty trophies, at least. Seven years of his life, right there. Each one's mounted on a piece of marble, a thin brass plaque with Josh's name chiseled in—the date written underneath it. Standing on top of every one is some faceless baseball player, swinging his bat. If you look close enough, you can see the runoff—that extra lip of plastic wrapped around the middle of his body, where the mold opened. Runs right down the center of him, over his chin, his chest—dividing him in half. They were cheap trophies, I know. Bought them myself, half the time, just to give the other kids something to feel proud about. Getting their names engraved was enough to set me back five bucks a teammate. But once we started making it to districts, the league had their own trophies. Big ones, too. Two columns instead of just one. A bigger chunk of marble. And a baseball player made out of brass. Real metal. Flick his head with your finger and his skull would ring like a tuning fork, the hum vibrating all the way through his bat—as if he'd just hit the biggest home run ever, striking that ball so hard, the knock echoed through his entire body, his own bones.

Josh earned two of those trophies. One for each time we went to the finals. He was so proud when he'd won them, he wouldn't put them down. Not for the entire day. We'd all go out for ice cream afterward, the whole team and their families. Josh just wouldn't let his trophy go. Gripping it by one of the columns, he balanced the base on his knee, eating his ice cream sundae with his free hand. I couldn't pry that thing away from him until he fell asleep later on that night, finding it hidden under his covers—he was hugging the trophy like a teddy bear. The brass was smudged with so many fingerprints. The baseball player's face had wrinkled over with streaks from Josh's greasy fingers. Had to polish him before putting the trophy onto the mantel with all the others. I got him to shine.

Whenever I lit a fire in the living room, those trophies would glow. They'd catch the flames and blaze, lighting up the whole room. Even the plastic ones brightened up, those miniature men looking like they were all burning. Playing baseball in hell, for all I know. Those trophies look more like tombstones to me now, each one engraved with its own special epitaph. *Joshua Raymond, The Delray Devils, 1985. Joshua Raymond, District All-Star Championships, 1991. Joshua Raymond, Born 1976. Died MVP, 1993.*

I can't remember what we even etched into his headstone anymore, but I can recite what it says on every trophy—word for word. Work my way up from his first prize at age nine, all the way to sixteen. Sixteen years old. There aren't any trophies after that. Not even a ribbon. Just enough wall space to count how many seasons Josh could've kept playing. Kept winning.

There had been five kids in the car when it crashed. I had coached three of them. Frank Partridge's boy. Kevin Winters. And Josh. I was the one who first taught them all how to pick up a grounder shuttling right at them, when they were only eight years old. You couldn't pick a kid on my team who I didn't consider to be a member of my family.

Save for Philip Winters's son. Kevin was the one who'd been driving that night. Ran their family van right off the highway. Not because any of them were drinking. Josh never touched the stuff during the season. Never got near anyone who did, either—

especially if they were driving. No, Kevin Winters was having an *asthma* attack. He wouldn't pull off the road to find his inhaler, stubborn enough to keep steering. Everyone in the neighborhood knew how ill that boy'd been. Bedridden for practically half of his life. I remember meeting him for the first time as some sickly kid signing up for the team, paler than the leather on the balls we were pitching. It didn't make sense why his mother would force him to play when it was pretty clear to me he didn't want to. The boy would throw such a fit before every practice, coughing his lungs out. He'd be wheezing before he even got up to bat. Nearly blew the ball right off the T with his breath alone. I had to tuck him into the outfield, as far away from the action as I could get him—just so he wouldn't be a hassle to the rest of the team.

I didn't have anything against the kid. Don't get me wrong. But we'd lose points because of him, *entire games*—no matter where I placed him on that field. He never learned how to catch. He'd stuff his inhaler somewhere in his glove, fumbling for it every time a pop fly came his way. He'd be sucking down his medicine when he should've been throwing the ball back to first base. That's why I placed Josh and him together in the first place. I figured, if I could put my son in between the ball and Kevin Winters, we wouldn't have to worry over losing another game ever again.

But with all that time alone in the outfield, Josh and Kevin started talking to each other. Started hanging out after practice. They became pals, growing up together. My son made captain of the high school baseball team by his freshman year, while Winters couldn't even keep up with his own lungs half the time.

You know, I've heard his parents knew he was having an asthma attack before he left the house that night—and they still let him drive. They allowed their son to get behind the wheel with all of our children in the car, while he just wheezed away, choking up on the highway until he swerved off the road. Busted through the guardrail and kept on going.

How much do you think Kevin's parents blamed themselves for what happened? Enough to drag them out here to these meetings with the rest of us? Not at all. They didn't want to mourn with the neighborhood. They hid in their home. They wouldn't even come out to our barbecues, either—even after Wendy would personally invite them. As a peace offering. As if it was *us* making amends to *them*, like it was our fault their boy killed our children.

You'd think they would've at least moved. Leave the neighborhood they'd tainted. But they kept to their house—a reminder to the rest of us over what we'd all lost.

What apologies did they give our families? Did Phil Winters ever say he was sorry for what his son had done to mine?

At Josh's service, you know what his teammates did for him? Anybody who ever played with him, from T-ball on up to high school, each one signed their name onto a different baseball, tossing them into the ground with his casket, like seeds scattered in with his body. Every time I go back to visit him, I think I'm going to find a tree growing out from his grave. Taking root into his body, I imagine that sapling would feed off of my son's suffering—sprouting out of the ground so strong, *so ready to play ball again*, that I could find some of Josh's bones stuck within its trunk. The tree would actually be enveloping him, lifting him out of his coffin.

And you know what I'd do? I'd cut that tree down, whittling into it. I'd make myself a bat out of my boy. Make one for every teammate of his, a regular Raymond Slugger for each of us. And we'd all play ball. That's what I'd do.

A lot of Josh's friends would visit me and Wendy, now and then. Even though they'd all grown out of T-ball a long time ago, they'd still call me coach. Saying *Mr. Raymond* just never sounded right, coming out from their mouths. I'd never been Mr. Raymond to any of them, never. Even after they'd moved onto playing baseball, I'd always be their coach—no matter who was training them now. Your son, Frank—I remember Jonathan and the guys coming over one day, and he said something like, "Do you want to toss the ball around a little, coach? For old times' sake?" We did, playing catch in my backyard. Felt so good to get this arm pitching again, tossing the ball to somebody. For just a moment, it really did feel like old times. Like Josh was just inside, getting his mitt.

I remember Ricky saying, "He could've made it to the majors, coach."

He could have. We all knew that.

Nearly half of our T-ball team is buried underground now. Shouldn't that make it easier for us? To think that they're all together, at least—starting up a league in the cemetery? With all of them lined up alongside each other like that, our children stuck in the dugout for good, a mound of dirt over each kid—they look like bases on a baseball field. Whenever I go alone, I can't help but make the rounds, running the headstones like I'd just hit a homer, sliding into each base just for the hell of it. Spence Partridge—*safe*. Kevin Winters—*safe*. And buried under home plate, my son—*Yeerrrr out!*

philip winters

"Better let me in, Delila. Your doorbell's going to crack if I keep ringing it like this. The plumbing's going to rupture soon, I swear. You're going to drown in there, if you don't open this door. Keep the chain fastened, if you have to. Just give me those three inches in between the chinks to see your face. I know there's someone on the other side of this door. I can almost make out your heartbeat pounding on the paneling. It's pulsing like a woodpecker, hammering through. That's got to be you, honey. I'd know that heart anywhere. There was a time when the only thing in between my hand and that pulse would've been a blanket or your blouse. Not some other house. Just like I couldn't live without my stomach or my liver, our home can't function without this family. That means the four of us. We're domestic intestines, keeping our household alive. I'm starting to see the sun come up. The newspaper boy just rode by on his bicycle. I can read the morning edition with one hand while the other keeps ringing the doorbell, if you're going to make me stay out here like this—all that racket resounding through the walls, running into the windows. Until the panes break. Until the glass shatters. I'll wake up this whole suburb, if I have to. The neighbors are already wondering why you won't let me in. Your own husband. I drove up all the way from Florida to see you—and you won't even look at me through the peephole."

Delila never unlocked the door, keeping the bolts in place, leaving us outside. When I told her you were with me; she finally spoke up, "Go home, Phil."

"But I am home. We finally made it."

"That's not our son. What you're carrying is not Kevin."

I'd take whatever I could get. Any little fragment was better than nothing. I'd been cheated out of hearing your voice break, that crack in your throat—your high-pitch crumbling away for a deeper sound. I didn't teach you how to shave, missing those first few whiskers springing from your chin. Your senior prom came and went without you. There's a gap in our photo albums, where you vanish right from the page—slipping away as if you just jumped off a canyon in our snapshots. Edey couldn't have been any older than eleven years old when you two last saw each other. You've probably begun to fade away from her mind already, falling out from her memory like her baby teeth—spit out and forgotten. The first week you were gone, we all kept close to the windows—holding our breath everytime a car turned onto our block. When the high beams would run over my face, I'd close my eyes, just to feel the warmth from the headlights over my skin, believing it was you.

And when that car would pass, I'd wait for the next one, then the next—willing to believe it over and over again, for as long as it took for you to pull into our driveway.

All of our attention went toward the doorbell, the telephone. Never to each other.

But then you came home, Kevin. Can you imagine what it felt like to say that? To actually have the words run up from my throat? *"Kevin's home,* honey," I said, banging my fists against Delila's door. I repeated it, "Kevin's home." There was honey rushing up from my heart, it felt so sweet to say it. I'd wanted those words for so long, starving myself for them, that once they finally filled my mouth, it was like tasting the flavor of family for the first time in years. I'd been famished for my loved ones to the point where I hadn't been able to eat anything else—not moving on, not forgetting, not trying to let go. I finally had my family back.

"I just called the police, Phil."

"Don't do this, Delila. Please."

"They'll be here in five minutes."

"Come with us. We can all hop in the car and go for a road trip. You, me, Edey, Kevin."

"I told them you would agree to leave if I asked you to. If you're still here when they pull in, Phil, they'll arrest you for assault."

I had always promised you a road trip. That's the one vow I've never let go of, Kevin—and now I was going to make good on that promise. Getting back into the car, I could see Delila in the window, peeking out. She was in her nightgown, her arms folded over her chest. A part of me wanted to believe she was just seeing me off to work, that I was waiting for a wave from the window before pulling out of the driveway.

They say eighty percent of the human body is comprised of water. That means you were drowning under your own skin from the very beginning, Kevin. Death was never farther than twenty percent away. *Eight tenths of your entire body.* That puts the surface somewhere around your neck, doesn't it? Your Adam's apple must've been bobbing above the water your whole life, marking where the rest of your body had gone down—everything below your throat wading through the muck of this pitiful existence. Your lungs kept you floating for as long as they could. You had a life preserver embedded in your chest, holding your head above water.

Too bad they were a faulty pair. There was a pop in your bronchial tubes, the air fizzing out for years. You wouldn't have lasted long, even if you hadn't had that car accident. Your lungs just weren't built for breathing. You were a fish out of water your whole life. Always gasping, your lips quivering for the right kind of air. If it hadn't been for your inhaler, you would've suffocated years ago—well before you ran the van off the road.

You were better off below, weren't you? I should've left you in the swamp, with all of your friends. Something tells me you were happier down there—dissolving into the water, your remains settling along the bottom of the van. The neighborhood gang really came together down there, didn't they? You, Josh and Mandy. Your best friend, Spence. Even Tamara tagged along. Your bodies had all blended together—your skin disintegrating, mixing into a morass all along the floor. There was no telling whose insides were whose anymore, everybody's organs coiling up together. We'd never be able to separate the lot of you from each other. Friends forever.

But what about you and me? When you were younger, you couldn't wait to get behind the wheel of your own car. I remember taking you to the shopping mall every Sunday morning, before the stores opened, giving you the run of the entire parking lot to practice your driving. We were the only people around, save for the seagulls picking through the litter. None of those birds would ever move, no matter how close you came to running them over. They'd grown accustomed to cars. They weren't afraid of some driver honking his horn anymore. Wasn't until they were six inches away from an incoming tire before the bird would even take flight, whipping out its wings at the last second, trying to take whatever piece of trash it had been pecking at along with him. Nothing but vultures, all of them. Without any traffic around, you could hear them squalling through the entire parking lot. Almost made me feel like we were at the beach again. We were miles away from the sea—and yet, here were all these gulls, carrying on as if the empty asphalt was their ocean, all gray and paved.

"All right. Let's trade places."

Putting the car in park, we'd switch seats. I'd sit shotgun while you slipped behind the wheel. You'd have to adjust the rearview mirror—scooting yourself up to the edge of the seat to reach the gas pedal. Before I'd let you turn on the ignition, we'd go through the rules of driving safely.

"What do you have to do before you even start the car?"

"Put on my seat belt."

"Have you done that yet?"

Reaching behind you, you brought the belt over your waist, buckling up, tethering your body back against the seat. "Okay."

"Is the car in park?"

"Yes."

"Can you see out of all your mirrors?"

You checked, glancing into each one—first the rearview, then the driver's side, then the passenger side. "Yes."

"How are we doing on gas?"

"Three quarters of a tank."

"Good. You ready, then?"

"Yeah."

"Okay, let's give it a whirl . . ."

The moment you twisted the key, the engine jumping to a start, it was as if your body had jolted into motion as well. The hum of the motor got you to grin, this look of excitement flowing over your face. The blood was even flushing into your cheeks, like oil flooding the engine, adding some color to your normally pale complexion.

"Give it some gas before you take it out of park, just so you can feel it rev up a bit."

Nodding, you pressed your foot down on the gas pedal. The sound of the engine strained itself, lifting up into a higher pitch. It frightened you at first, the car was growling at you. You took your foot off fast. Either your asthma was stirring or your seat belt was on too tight, but suddenly your breathing had become thick, labored. By reflex, you pulled out your inhaler and took a puff—easing your breath down, steadying itself with the engine.

"It's okay, Kevin. The car's not going anywhere until you put it into drive. Just try it again."

Taking another hit from your inhaler, you pressed the pedal down, letting the engine slowly accelerate. The motor gently hummed up into a higher octave, nearly purring by the time the pedal was touching the floor. The tips of your lips lifted up into another grin, your eyes catching sparks. Turning to me, you asked, "Can I drive now, Dad?"

"Ready whenever you are."

You slipped the car out of park and into drive, the transmission seizing the wheels and sending us forward. Your foot went for the brake, the sudden halt in our momentum pushing us toward the dashboard. I almost slammed my head against the glove compartment.

"Sorry . . ."

"It's okay. I'm not expecting perfection here. Just take it slow."

You promptly nodded. I'd never seen you so attentive before. You were hanging off my every word, actually listening to what I said.

The seagulls stood at attention as we fumbled through the parking lot, our car repeatedly stopping and starting every few yards, sending a series of these abrupt spurts of screeching tires into the air. It sounded like a trumpet blurting out random notes, beckoning the neighboring birds to squawk back.

Eventually, you got a feel for the wheel—warming up to the car, how it drove. We spent hours just going in circles. By the time the parking lot started to fill up with other automobiles, you could steer around the entire shopping mall on your own. The windshield was covered in seagull droppings by the end of the morning—white strips dribbling down the glass, speckling your visibility.

I don't think I'd ever seen you so happy before. There was this electricity inside your eyes that I don't know if I'd ever found at any other time. Getting you behind the wheel was as much of a gift to me as it probably was for you.

"How am I doing, Dad?"

"Doing just fine. You're doing great." I couldn't remember you ever asking for my approval before.

This car was where we connected best, I believed. I wouldn't worry over your asthma and you wouldn't close up on me. All of our arguments dissolved. When we buckled up, we were invincible.

"When I get my driver's license, Dad, do you think we could go on a road trip or something? Just you and me?"

"Where would you like to go?"

"I don't know. Anywhere, I guess."

"Is there any place that you'd really like to see?"

"I've never been outside of the South before. Could we like, go to New York or something?"

"New York would be fun. Sure."

"Really?"

"Why not? How about this summer?"

"You really want to?"

"Yeah, let's go. Just you and me."

"And we can split up the driving? I get half and you get half?"

"Of course. I'll navigate for you when you're behind the wheel and you'll navigate for me when I'm behind the wheel."

"Yeah!" Putting the car back into park, you turned the ignition off, yanked out the keys, and then handed them back to me. Dropped them right into the palm of my hand. My fingers wrapped around the keys and I squeezed, their metal teeth digging into my skin.

That was the last time we ever talked about traveling together. The summer of your sixteenth birthday came and went. You took your driver's test and passed, bringing home your temporary license the very same day. The photo they slapped onto that I.D. card was the last picture anyone ever took of you. I remember it, how excited you looked. Somehow the snapshot had captured this electricity surging up in your eyes, your irises a pair of spark plugs about to catch. The second the bulb flashed, that camera may have caught the happiest moment of your life. The DMV had given you the freedom to drive, there was nothing holding you back from hitting the highway.

When it came time for you to ask if you could borrow the van, wanting to drive your friends to the movies or wherever you were supposed to go, I couldn't allow myself to say yes, to let you enter onto this interstate.

"You know I'm a good driver," you said. "You taught me yourself."

"It's not your driving that I'm worried about, Kevin. It's the other people on the road."

"So, what? Now that I've gotten my license, I can't use it? That's not fair."

"I'm not trying to be fair. I'm trying to be safe."

"Mom—"

"Listen to your breathing, Kevin. You're about to have another asthma attack."

"I'm going out, whether you let me or not! I'm tired of staying in my room."

The urge to drive off was always in you. Didn't matter where or with who, you simply itched for that escape. I bet you didn't even have a reason to run away. It was just ingrained in your system, this inherent need to leave. Guess that makes you some kind of salmon. You just needed the means to swim upstream, hitting this highway and driving as far away from Florida as you could. Away from me. Your whole life was bent toward reaching that final destination, a place where you could die.

I just wanted to come pick you up. Bring you back home.

But right now the only home we have is this car. The road will be our backyard. We'll just keep driving until we find a safe place to settle. We just passed another family. They may as well be our neighbors now. The road's been littered with children all day. There was a boy in the backseat of that last car, making him the fifth kid I've seen within the past five miles. His face was pressed up against the window, blowing out his cheeks at me. His lips were squirming over the glass, spread open enough for me to see the inside of his mouth. That tender tongue. When I watched that inch's worth of window fog over with his breath, the air in between his lips thickening—I thought I was looking at you. That boy could've been you.

Suddenly I saw the van sinking into the swamp, just as if it were happening in front of me. I imagined the moment all over again. You were still behind the steering wheel. Your hands were pushing against the glass, your palms pressed flat across the window. I could see the water seeping inside the car—the surface rising up to your chest, reaching for your throat. You had your eyes on me the entire time, locked onto mine—the two of us staring at each other as the water touched your chin. You took in a deep breath before the surface lifted over your lips. You kept staring at me, until the water had risen over your eyes, blurring your vision. One moment, you knew exactly where I was. The next, you'd lost me. The water washed away your vision, all the shapes and sharp edges surrounding you dissolving away. There was nothing for you to look at anymore. Everything had gone boggy.

You still had your seat belt on. You never took it off. The thought must've never crossed your mind. If you had just reached over and unbuckled yourself, you could've drifted away.

You looked confused. Your lips kept curling into question marks, as if you wanted to ask me something while still trying to keep the air in.

Then your breath began to slip. Just a couple bubbles at first, one or two every few seconds. Then more, your lungs suddenly beginning to boil. Your breath had become too hot to hold on to any longer, the bubbles sputtering up from your lips like steam whistling through a teakettle. Your eyes widened as this chain of air percolated out from the corner of your mouth, each link rolling over your cheek.

The pressure on your lungs was lessening. Your chest was deflating. Your body was sinking back into your seat, the belt slackening its tension around your waist. But your eyes kept searching for me, cutting through the water—desperate to find my fuzzy face on the other side of the van's window. You kept hammering your hands over the window, desperate for the oxygen on the other side. Your body had become a fishing pole, your lungs casting the old air out—hooked onto the hopes of breathing. But you couldn't reel a fresh breath back in. Oxygen had become the one that'd gotten away.

The urge to just open your mouth had gotten so strong. Everything within you was beginning to shrivel, your body begging for a breather. Just a nibble of air.

So when your teeth parted, your jaw dropping open—it was enough of an invitation for the water to rush right in, hounding the hollow of your lungs and swelling your chest. The shock of cold widened your eyes. The jolt of water rushing down your windpipe sent your body buckling forward. I've imagined the spasms so many times, pictured your limbs whipping through the water. You lift your head up, extending your throat until your Adam's apple bulged out as far as your neck would allow. It bobbed along your esophagus, ducking under your skin, then rising back up again—as if your line had finally hooked something. Something big. Something you couldn't reel back in on your own. Something that would yank your fishing pole right out of your hands. Something that would pull you into the water if you didn't let go.

Something that would cure your respiratory problems once and for all. You'd never need an inhaler down there, that's for sure. Your asthma wouldn't bother you, ever again—the need to breathe was all washed away.

I keep seeing you drown, son. Every time we pass a child on the highway, it's *you* there—wrestling with the water, the inside of the car filling up. I have to relive your lungs swelling up with water. I have to see you suck in that swamp a thousand times. Just when the bubbles stop sputtering and your body goes limp, there's a second of you simply drifting in your seat, tethered down by the belt.

You are so still. Your lips are always parted.

And then you look up at me. Your head lifts up and you find me for the first time since your eyes went underwater, as if they had just adjusted to the light. We'll look at each other for as long as our cars are aligned with one another, side by side in our neighboring lanes.

Then when you drive past, another car will take your place. If there's a kid sitting in the backseat, it starts up all over again. It's as if the water drained out from the van, only to refill for me once more. I get to watch the windows fill up, the air thin out—as if it's happening for the first time. For the hundredth time today. You'll always be drowning for me, Kevin. Your lungs will always welcome in the water.

Now it's time to pull over, rest for a while. I've been holding on to this road like a child clinging to his mother's leg. I've got to let go of this steering wheel for a little bit, get the feeling back into my fingers again.

miss corpus

Congratulations. It's a girl. Pulling me off the shelf was an act of parturition—you know that? You just delivered your own baby, doc. And look at the handful you got. The moment you opened this book I ushered in my first breath, the air slipping past these pages and filling them up to the margins. There's life within these lungs now. Hot off the press.

Feel that? Flip through me fast enough and you can feel my exhales spreading across your face, the air breezing past your cheeks. That's me. I'm breathing. I can even sense my blood flowing from one sentence to the next, every letter its own little capillary carried through the verbose veins of my body.

But you can't cram me back into that crack on the bookshelf anymore. I wouldn't fit. That cervix will seal itself up with another book before too long, this uterus always stocked up with enough copies to keep spitting out kids for all these other customers. Whether you knew what you were getting into or not, you've just travailed your own child. I'm so small, I can fit right in the palm of your hand—the binding of my spine running up the length of your fingers, my tailbone resting against your wrist. You can snip the umbilical cord at the cash register up front. They'll even let you pocket the placenta as a proof of purchase, that receipt saying I'm all yours.

Feel how smooth this skin is? That book jacket's as velvety as a newborn's behind. No creases, no dog-eared pages. No wrinkles whatsoever. You couldn't find a misprint within me, if you tried. My entire body's blue until you give me that first slap on the back and crack my cover wide open—letting the air in, letting the blood flow. And reading me. Getting to the heart of what I have to say—the words circulating through my body, cover to cover. You're raising me within your imagination. Your eyes are my lifeblood, every turn of the page another pulse perusing through my body. The deeper you read into me, the older I'll grow. I'll pass through puberty after the first chapter.

I'm lucky enough to be coming from a wonderful family. My father's an author. Guess that makes him my fauthor (*ha-ha*). You know who my mother is. Probably even passed by her a couple times before yourself. She's the South—a stretch of states so pretty, she inspired my dad to write me down. Now how romantic is that? Being born in the Blue Ridge Mountains, it was as if destiny had brought the two of them together—my father delivered right into Virginia's arms. He wooed her for years. He wrote for *her*. They'd spend hours on end in his room, alone. He'd be bound to his desk, mounting the South. When they made love, there was nothing beyond the two of them. Every border and county line closed in with her embrace, holding him against her body. The lower part of this country would contract, clinging onto my father. Her heart would start racing so fast, you could see the veins in her neck throbbing—the interstates flushed with a sudden rush of blood. The air trapped between their bodies would heat up, the humidity rising high—thickening into this sweat that stuck to just about everything. You could even feel it in your throat when you'd try to breathe.

They'd end up writing the night away. With all those characters swarming through his head, their voices like sperm anxious for their release—he made love to my mother as if she were a blank sheet of paper just waiting to be written all over. Something always made its way to the page, soaking up the sheets in their sweaty sex—staining the bedspread with a patch of paragraphs or some specks of sentences. The thrusts of his pelvis punctuated my mother's open fields, like tapping at a typewriter—a bell ringing every time she reached the end of a line, orgasming on down to a new column.

Tick, tick, tick, tick, tick—*bing!* tick, tick, tick, tick, tick, tick—*bing!* tick, tick, tick, tick, tick, tick, tick, *bing!* For hours.

I'll ask my dad, *What was Mom like when she was my age?* and he'll reply, *Just like you*. Something about that always makes me happy, no matter how many times I've heard him say it. I'm just like my mother. To hear him talk of their love together is to bear witness to history. I should know. I get to embody it. I'm a living, breathing testimonial. There had been hope of them having a baby for a long, long time. My father was much younger than my mother. He'd never written a novel before. There'd been a couple literary miscarriages between the two of them, a few aborted book ideas along the way. Neither of them talk about that. Either out of shame or pain or just plain self-preservation, you'll never hear a word of it from them.

But they kept trying. My father figured, you could take the boy out of the South but you couldn't take the South out of the boy. He felt the need to rear a bright-eyed, rosy-cheeked tome that could encapsulate his one and only love. A living, breathing monument to my mother. I-95 would be the umbilical cord between us, nurturing me. Seems like I got my mother's good looks. Her blue eyes, her stately frame. While from my father, I guess I have to make do with his mouth. I sound like him sometimes—which can be pretty scary. Guess that's what you get for taking after your father. Daddy's little girl and all.

He must've seen this day coming. I'd enter into the world alone, leaving him and Mom behind. Now that I'm on my own, he's got nothing but an empty nest left in his head—strained of a year's worth of writing, his imagination drained to the last drop. But I bet you they have another baby before too long. I'll have me a brother or a sister soon enough. This will be a big family.

It's funny. They say that when you die, your entire life flashes in front of your eyes within that final second. Every moment you've ever experienced comes barreling through your brain all over again. Memories you'd forgotten you even had come rising up, reminding you of times you would've lost otherwise. You relive everything within that one last gasp of air.

Guess I went about it the opposite way. I was born with a head full of memories that I haven't even experienced yet. My life was mapped out for me before I even had the chance to breathe. Every moment I'm destined to live has already been pinpointed for me, marked down onto an atlas of my own existence—simply waiting for me to make it on time. Recollections come to me in a car wreck, where everybody slows down to see what happened. Parts of my past crash into each other, muddling up my memory with so many awkward thoughts, mismatched moments. I remember being conceived in between two bending fenders just outside of Sumter, South Carolina. Traffic on I-95 had been steady in both the south- and northbound lanes, the opposing current of cars flowing smoothly alongside one another. A clot of road construction near Kingstree thickened the flux heading west, redirecting a rush of automobiles down highway 378. The surge would end up merging with the interstate in less than twenty miles. Other than that, the roadway was calm. Sumter had a crown of turnpikes rising up from its city limits—highways 521, 15, and 75 all converging just next to the main drag, diffusing the number of cars clumping together. Each exit funneled down the amount of traffic, letting every cluster of caravans move freely. It was smooth sailing from here to Waterloo.

The highway hummed with over a hundred running engines, a hive of cars coalescing with one another—families on vacation, kids taking their first road trip, drifters hitching a ride elsewhere. William Colby's windshield had fogged over with the dust and dirt of countless days of travel, caked in enough exhaust to leave the glass looking cataracted—going blind to the highway. Sleep was seeping into his body, the urge to turn off taking over. He flipped on the turn signal, the blinker's pulse throbbing through his own veins. The posted speed limit was sixty-five miles an hour. Looking at the speedometer, he realized he was going ninety-seven. The steering wheel leaned to the left, the car drifting onto the median. The smoothness of the asphalt was replaced with grass. Will could hear the soft scrape of foliage slipping over the underbelly of his car, like Shelly's hair brushing across his face.

Philip Winters's hands kept slipping off his steering wheel. He was too tired to even keep his grip, his fingers easing free every five minutes. All he wanted was to pull off. Turning the steering wheel to his left, gravel spit up underneath the chassis. Then the sound went soft, the tires running through the grass. Phil's neck loosened, tilting back against the headrest.

Will found the front of an oncoming car filling his vision. A station wagon. He had a second to recognize the model, to see the man sitting behind the wheel. There was a moment between them, a breath to behold each other before colliding. The air went in and never came back out.

Phil found the front of an oncoming car filling his vision. A Honda. He had a second to recognize the model, to see the man sitting behind the wheel. There was a moment between them, a breath to behold each other before colliding. The air went in and never came back out.

The momentum behind each automobile adhered them together, their grilles like two sets of gritted teeth grinding against the other. A ripple shook through their hoods, the metal softened by the impact, sending a shiver through their steel cheeks. Will was thrust up against his steering wheel. The rim crushed his larynx, his Adam's apple halving itself under the pressure. His seat belt reeled him back, his body volleyed between the wheel and headrest over and over again. The coolers cracked open upon impact. Water washed over his back, a warm rush running down his neck. His car had sprung a leak, his boat sinking fast. *Women and children first,* he thought. And since it's said that the captain always goes down with his ship, Will let Shelly go—watching her slip out through the windshield while he stayed inside the car. This boat had been begging to go to the bottom for days now, drifting through enough countryside to flounder down in Florida. It was only a matter of time before the tires popped. Will was ready to anchor his automobile down, dragging his ship into the ditch, where he could sink with a sense of solitude. The water was still with him, even out here. He believed the body rushing in through his windshield was really the sea, a tidal wave of limbs washing over him. He took in a mouthful of the man, opening his throat for the ocean to come flooding through.

Phil was whisked through his window, whipped into a flip, his entire body sent over backward in the air. There was a moment of coasting, his body floating over the ground. He landed on the windshield of the other car, shattering through the glass. Holding his breath, Phil slid in as if to dive into a body of water. His eyes were unaccustomed to the muck of another man's car, slipping beneath the surface of the windshield—only to find another body floating below, tethered down by the seat belt. It was a young man, around the age that Kevin could've been if he were still alive—his limbs drifting in the air from the force of impact. He had just jumped into the swamp that had swallowed Kevin up, discovering his body below. He embraced his boy before finally letting go.

Will and Phil welcomed themselves into each other's arms like old friends. The force of impact snapped Will's neck back, while Phil's chest collapsed against the steering wheel. The sound of tires scraping against the pavement hailed the occasion, the two cars careening off the road and into the ditch.

The two of them tumbled into the thickets by the side of the road, garnished with the limbs and bits of their loved ones. With the life he had left within him, Phil looked to his side to find Will bubbling up his breath. He couldn't help but grin, realizing this man looked nothing like his son. The thought made him laugh, which hurt his ribs—but he continuing to giggle anyway. Will opened his eyes, only to see this man hacking up blood all over his face.

"What's so funny?" Will asked.

"I'm supposed to be on a road trip with my son."

"Where's your son?"

"He couldn't make it."

Will's left eye rolled upward without his right eye following, looking toward his car. His lips peeled back in a smile, his teeth smeared red.

"What's so funny to you?" Phil asked.

"I'm supposed to be on my honeymoon."

"Oh yeah? Where's your wife?"

"She stayed at home."

They both laughed, the sound of traffic washing away their voices.

All the other automobiles driving by had begun to slow down, easing up on the gas pedal just enough to see what had happened. Passengers ogled the accident, transfixed by this image of bodies by the side of the highway.

"Honey, turn your head the other way. Don't look out there."

From the backseat of his parents' car, one boy focused on the pile of mismatched limbs. He saw a man's face staring up into the air. His mouth hung open, closing slightly every few seconds, only to slacken again, refusing to keep shut. Beside him was another man, lying facedown in the ditch. His neck had almost twisted completely toward his back, his chin resting against his right shoulder blade. The boy rolled down his window to get a better look, squinting as the distance between him and the wreck grew.

"Say a prayer for those poor people, honey," his mother said, shaking her head from the front seat.

I'll grow up knowing where I've come from once you reach my last chapter. I'll be able to count the number of breaths left for me by how many pages you turn through. And once you're rushing through that final sentence, the words fading away, we'll have reached the end together. But right now, right here—when you read me, I can feel my heart beating. This is the life you give me. You've reached beyond my ribs, burrowed below my binding. You've cradled me in the cup of your hands and felt the pulse pushing through. Put a finger over each cover, front and back, and spread my legs wide open. You'll be my first. My one and only.

Sounds like a good read to me.

Acknowledgments

Without these people, I honestly have no idea where I would be right now. They deserve more credit than I can ever give. For my amazing agent, Heide Lange—who made all of this possible. For my editor, Peternelle van Arsdale—who chiseled this chunk of words into a novel. To Natalie Kaire and everyone at Hyperion. To Esther Sung and everyone at Sanford J. Greenburger Associates. Thank you for believing in me. Let me continue to make you proud.

To my mentors, from the sixth grade on up—Susan Royer, Randy Strawderman, John Moon, Katherine Baugher, Peter Raimist, Robert Moyer, Tanya Belov, Brooke Stevens, Regina Arnold, Frank Golden, Tom Molloy, Martin Healy, Ed Baker, and Victoria Redel. Thank you for teaching me to go against the grain.

For opening a door when no one else would—Erez Ziv and Kimo DeSean. Thank you for the opportunity to do something important.

For their patience and faith, but ultimately for their friendship—Joshua Camp and Michael Hearst. Thank you for sticking around for so long.

For everything I've never acknowledged them for, for all the thanks I never gave—my family, Sue Henshaw, Joe Campbell, Gail and Rob Patrick, Bill and Suze Henshaw. Thank you for raising me exactly the way you did.